STAR WIND

STAR WIND

Linda Woolverton

Houghton Mifflin Company
Boston 1986

Library of Congress Cataloging-in-Publication Data

Woolverton, Linda.
  Starwind.

  Summary: Camden returns from a month at camp to find
her best friend and other classmates frighteningly
changed and devoted to a mysterious young man named WT-3.
  [1. Science fiction]   I. Title.
PZ7.W88715St   1986   [Fic]   85-31727
ISBN 0-395-41454-7

Printed in the United States of America

S   10 9 8 7 6 5 4 3 2 1

To Ida Jane
For the Ducks and all the Birthday Cakes

Contents

STAR WIND

ʃ

1

Clean Sheets

CAMDEN DOUGLAS threw her dusty sleeping bag into her room and flopped down onto the bed. She wasn't happy about being home. Summer camp had been too much fun. She felt out of place in the neat tidiness of her room after a whole month in a dusty bungalow. She noticed her dirty footprints that tracked across the beige carpet.

It's too clean almost, she thought to herself.

Camden's mother had asked her to take a bath and get ready for dinner. But she didn't want to wash away that wonderful woodsy, outdoor feeling, not yet. Camden ran her hand over the smooth clean sheets on her bed. She did have to admit that they were going to feel cool and comfortable after that musty old sleeping bag.

I guess being home isn't so bad after all, she thought.

Besides, Camden had lots of hard-earned camp stories to tell her friend Mitch, Mitch Malkovich. She loved to say both his names together. She could say "Mitch Malkovich" ten times fast without a single mistake and he couldn't.

Mitch lived three houses down on Camden's block in a two-story house with a pool and big brothers and a real trampoline. She liked him because he was smart and he could always make her laugh. Mitch's ears stuck straight out, his hair sometimes looked kind of funny, and he got sunburned way too easily, but Camden guessed he was her best friend. Aside from Maggie, of course.

One of the best things about Maggie was that she answered whenever Camden called. She could be anywhere, even down the block, and if Camden listened really hard she could always hear the small voice calling back. Every night Maggie would curl into a neat little cat ball on the foot of Camden's bed. Sometimes they would share secrets way into the night.

Camden got up and went downstairs to find her cat. But Maggie wasn't in any of the usual places. She looked on top of the dryer. She looked in her dad's chair in the study. She looked in the sunny spot on the kitchen floor.

"Mom," Camden asked, "have you seen Maggie?"

"No, not since this morning," her mother answered as she struggled with some brittle uncooked pasta shells. Mrs. Douglas was making a welcome-home dinner of Camden's favorite things: real mashed potatoes (not that fake flake stuff), creamed corn (out of a can), and cannelloni, a great Italian dish that Camden always ordered in restaurants.

The cannelloni was giving her mom a little trouble. She had been learning to cook for the past ten years. She said it made her nervous. Even though Mrs. Douglas had been to college, taught English at Santa Monica High, and sold real estate on weekends, she had trouble cooking more than one thing at a time.

"Well, I can't find her," Camden complained.

"She'll show up," her mom answered. "Now will you help me put this cheese stuff in these shells? If I break one more I'm going to throw the whole mess out the window!"

Just then Maggie breezed into the kitchen. She ignored Camden completely.

"Maggie, aren't you glad to see me?" Camden asked in a hurt voice.

But Maggie only gave her a stuck-up glare in reply.

"Maggie, now just quit it! Did you miss me or not?" Camden pleaded. This time Maggie answered, but the reply was short and snotty.

"Maw," she said. Then she sat down and calmly began licking her leg.

"What's the matter with her, Mom?" Camden asked.

Her mother brushed a stray hair back from her forehead.

"Oh, she's still mad at you for going away, I think. If I didn't know better I'd say she was just trying to make you feel guilty."

"Well," Camden answered, "I don't feel guilty one bit and I think she's just being mean on purpose."

Her mother shrugged. "A cat's a cat, what can you say?"

Later that night, Camden and her parents sat on the floor in the living room and played their regular weekly game of Scrabble. Usually Maggie would come and sit on Camden's lap during the game. But tonight she pranced right past them without even so much as a glance and sat on top of her scratching post. She stared out the window, chattering at the pigeons.

"So," Camden's father said. "Read any good books lately?"

Both of her parents were big on books. They said that reading opened doors to the imagination and stretched the mind. Camden didn't think she'd want her mind stretched, but she loved to read. It was fun, at camp, to make a little tent of her sleeping bag and read by flashlight when everyone else was fast asleep.

"Well," she answered, "I finished all the books I took with me and somebody forgot to send me any more."

She gave her mom a sideways look.

"Sorry, honey," her mother answered. "I guess I just got busy and forgot."

Her father glanced up. "What about the camp library?" he asked.

"Oh, they didn't have anything good," Camden answered. "Just little kids' books and teen magazines, stuff like that. But I scrounged around and found an old copy of *The Jungle Books*. So I started reading it all over again."

"And who wrote *The Jungle Books*?" her father asked.

This was a test. He always insisted that Camden remember the authors of all the books she read.

She sighed. "Kipling, something Kipling."

"Rudyard," he said and placed his Scrabble letters to read JUNGLE.

"Remember the story about Rikki-Tikki-Tavi, the mongoose, who attacks that huge cobra?" Camden spelled TIGER on the board.

"I liked the Mowgli stories best," her mother told them, spelling WOLVES with her tiles.

Camden and her family didn't just play regular Scrabble. They had their own family version, and part of it was to come up with words that fit into whatever they were talking about. Even though they used extra tiles, this made the game twice as hard. Her father said the challenge was good for her. Camden wasn't so sure. Sometimes she felt the same way about "challenge" as she felt about "stretching the mind."

"So anyway," Camden added, "I'd love to have a mongoose around the house. Dad," she said loudly, hoping that Maggie would overhear her, "if Maggie doesn't start being nice to me, can we get a mongoose instead?"

But Maggie acted as though she couldn't care less. She gave Camden an offended look, then turned back to her pigeons.

"So what else did you do at camp?" her father asked.

"Mmmm, let's see. I wrote you about the overnight sleep-outs and the talent show and winning second place in the swim meet and —"

"It's your turn, Camden," her mother interrupted.

She had to stop talking long enough to figure out what word to spell with her letters. Camden finally came up with MARSHMALLOW.

"I take it you roasted those over the campfire?" her mother asked.

"Right," she answered. "And I rode this big white stallion. He was really hard to handle but they let me ride him anyway."

"Did you make any new friends?" her dad asked, spelling PALOMINO with his letters.

"Yes, but nobody like Mitch," Camden told him. "See, there was this one girl who was a real baby and she had just got a tetanus shot in her arm and she whined about it all day long and we played jokes on her and—"

"And I notice that you haven't taken your bath yet the way I asked you to," her mother said as she spelled BUBBLES on the game board.

"Oh, pretty soon," Camden answered.

"I think maybe *now* is more like it, young lady," her mother informed her.

"Aw, Mom," Camden complained. "We haven't even finished the game yet!"

It was her father's turn. He looked at Camden, smiled a big smile, and spelled SCRAM with his letters.

She laughed. "Nope, sorry, Dad. You can't use slang in this game."

He groaned and threw a sofa pillow at her.

So Camden had to take a bath after all. Usually Maggie sat on the edge of the tub while Camden bathed. She would watch over her very carefully as if she were worried that Camden might drown. But on that first night home from camp, Maggie didn't show up for the entire bath. Camden finally gave up and went to bed, but Maggie didn't follow. She called her one last time; no answer.

"Fine! Be that way," Camden grumbled and turned out the light.

A long time later, there was a small scratch at the door. Then a thin stream of light shone down upon a sleek, gray figure. Stepping lightly across the blankets, Maggie curled up tight next to her sleeping friend.

Camden's drowsy hand reached out to pull her closer.

"It's about time," Camden mumbled and they both fell asleep.

2

Something's Different Here

AT MITCH'S front door the next day, Camden got that tingly sensation in her stomach. It was exactly like that moment right before the roller coaster plunges straight down into nothingness. She was excited because she hadn't seen her best friend in over a month and she had a zillion things to tell him about camp. Besides, she said to herself, I just want to plain ol' see him because I missed his stupid face. Maggie was perched on the fence at above-dog height.

When the door opened, two huge black Labradors burst out, almost knocking Camden over in a wild attempt to reach her cat. Maggie pretended not to notice. But she really loved to tease them.

Camden started talking the minute Mitch opened the door.

"Haven't you taught those dogs any manners yet? I had a great time at camp, you should have been there, and I won second place in the swim meet and I rode this great horse and—" She stopped in midsentence. "Mitch! You look awful!"

He never actually got a real tan, but even in the heart of winter Mitch never looked this pale.

"You look like a sick fish. What happened?" she asked.

He leaned against the door, not acting very sick at all.

"Camden," he said, "double good to see your unit."

"Huh?" she said.

"Double good," he repeated.

Camden didn't know what to say. She remembered the last time she had seen him. It was the night before she left for camp. Mitch had loaned her his sleeping bag and his Swiss Army knife, his special waterproof watch, and a stack of tattered paperback books. Camden had been standing on the porch trying to hold all the stuff in her arms. She remembered that he kept running back into the house to get something else to add to the pile. Finally he had come out with his brand-new twenty-five-dollar underwater mask. He had never even worn it once. Mitch had put it on her face and laughed at how stupid she would look walking home with the mask on.

That had been a month ago. Now he was standing in the very same door, but he seemed different. It wasn't really the way he looked. He was acting funny—not exactly unfriendly, just not the way a best friend should act.

"Uh, yeah," she finally managed to mumble. There was a long moment of unfamiliar silence between them before Camden started all over.

"So, Mitch, how've you been and what've you been doing all summer?"

"Hanging with the Kidsters and WT-3," he answered, as if she knew exactly what he was talking about.

Is he kidding or what? she asked herself. Camden decided to play along just in case this was all a big joke.

"Oh, sounds fun. What's a WT-3?" she asked.

"You'll see," he answered secretively, then started pulling his dogs back into the house.

"Wanna help me with these droolers?"

"Droolers?" she asked, confused for a moment. "Oh! The dogs! Droolers." Camden chuckled. "That's funny, Mitch."

But he wasn't smiling as he tried to get the dogs away from Maggie. Mitch's Labs always went crazy around her. For some reason she just drove them nuts. Maggie liked to make long leaps from the fence to the trees and back again, just to drive the dogs crazy. The Labradors would jump and snap as she soared close to their open jaws. But they could never jump quite high enough. Camden thought Maggie lived a little too dangerously.

They finally got both dogs back into the house. Then Mitch slammed the front door and grabbed his bike, which he always kept parked on the porch.

"Lezgo," he said, bouncing the wheels down the steps. He was off before Camden could blink twice.

"Lezgo?" she repeated. Camden had never heard him say that before. Frowning, she ran to her bike and rushed to catch up.

"Wait up, Mitch! Where are we going?" she asked, pedaling beside him.

"To WT-3's," he answered, as if she should already know.

"Where?" she asked.

He gave her an annoyed look. "WT-3's!"

"Okay," she said. "Don't get mad. I'd just like to know where we're going."

Boy, Camden thought, is he touchy!

They rode in silence down the quiet, tree-lined summer streets. But when Mitch turned down Ocean Boulevard and started south, Camden began to get worried.

"Uh, Mitch," she asked, "where does this WT person live?"

"Venice," he answered.

"Oh, great!" she announced, screeching to a halt.

Venice is a little arty town just south of Santa Monica, next to the beach. And because Santa Monica was Camden's home town, Venice was naturally much more fun. Besides, it is full of artists and musicians and actors and surfer types. Young and old all live tightly packed together as close as they can get to the water. The boardwalk in Venice is like a circus all year round. There are street vendors and musclemen, roller skaters and skateboarders, people wearing bright colors and strange clothes. Camden liked Venice because it reminded her of what an olden-times town square would be like. There are even bums leaning against lampposts and talking to themselves and old bag ladies with their shopping carts full of dirty rags.

However, the very things that made Venice so exciting

for kids also made all the parents in Santa Monica very nervous. But living so close, they knew they would never keep their kids out of there. So very strict rules about going to Venice were made: only in daytime, never alone, and only after special permission was granted.

"Mitch, why didn't you tell me?" she complained. "Now my mom's going to be mad because I didn't ask permission!"

His brakes squeaked as he jerked his bike to a stop.

"So?" he asked.

"So!" Camden was getting annoyed. "So I wish you would have told me! My parents have rules about Venice. You know that!"

"Grownie rules," he snorted and took off again.

Camden leaned against her handlebars, staring after him. Grownie rules? What was that supposed to mean? This was a Mitch she had never seen before. She was certain now. Even though he looked just the same, Mitch had changed somehow while she was gone.

There was something going on here that Camden didn't like one bit.

Camden jumped back on her bike. She pedaled as fast as she could to catch up.

"Mitch, wait up!" she yelled, pulling up beside him.

"All right, I'll go," she said. "But I have to call home the minute we get there."

He looked over and smiled.

"Double good."

3

The (Something) View Arms

*T*HEY PEDALED along the bike path down Ocean Boulevard, weaving in and out of the parked cars. Camden loved this ride. The sea breeze blew against her face and she raised her arms to ride with no hands. Looking out over the water, Camden had the feeling that she was flying free into forever.

As they entered Venice, the streets got smaller and the two bike riders had to be more careful of cars and pedestrians. They were forced to stop several times and wait for whole crowds of sun-bathers to cross the street.

"Sand lizards!" Mitch commented under his breath.

The houses began to look more run-down as they rode farther south. But Camden liked the buildings here because they were brightly painted with odd colors. Some of the warehouses even had huge pictures painted on them that made it seem as if the street continued right on through the building. When Camden went to Venice, she always felt as though she were entering a patchwork town.

"Are we about there or what?" she called over to Mitch after they had pedaled about a mile.

For an answer he turned onto a side street and pulled his bike up to the front of a very old, broken-down three-story building. Camden didn't think it looked like anybody's house.

"Get serious!" she said, laughing. "I hate to tell you this, Mitch, but nobody's lived here for a long time."

The decrepit building had a faded sign hanging above the boarded-up front door. Camden could barely make out two of the three words, (Something) View Arms.

"Mitch, you have totally lost it! This looks like one of those hotels where old people hang out. Only this place is so old, the *old* people have left!" She laughed at her joke.

Ignoring her comments, Mitch parked his bike near the side of the building. But Camden didn't have a kickstand, and by the time she finally got her bike to lean against the stucco wall, Mitch had disappeared.

"Mitch?" she called. "Mitch?"

Camden walked cautiously along the side of the old hotel. Suddenly she didn't like being there.

"Okay, Mitch, this isn't funny. Now come on out!"

But he didn't appear, laughing, from around a corner, the way she expected.

"Mitch?" she called again, quietly.

Without warning, something cold grabbed her ankle. But Camden didn't scream. Her mom had taught her not to scream. She just stood frozen, eyes clenched shut, waiting for the horrible monster to finish her off.

"Camden."

It was Mitch. He had climbed down some stairs leading to a basement and stuck his hand out the low window to catch her as she went by.

Camden breathed a sigh of relief.

"Thanks a lot, Mitch. Not funny."

This whole day was beginning to get on her nerves. She went down the stairs and squeezed through an opening in a locked door that didn't look as though it was supposed to be squeezed through.

There was darkness inside, darkness and a musty smell like dirty gym clothes.

"Mitch?" she whispered, straining to see in the dark. "Mitch!" she repeated. "I'm getting sick of this now! Are you here or not?"

Just then a dim shaft of light snaked down a flight of stairs to reveal her friend standing at the top, profiled against the doorway.

"Lezgo," he said impatiently and she scurried after him, bumping into things so odd she didn't even want to know what they were.

The stairs opened into a dusty hallway, but there was a little more light to see by. As she followed Mitch, Camden's eyes slowly adjusted to the dimness. She could see torn, stained wallpaper peeling off in faded layers to reveal even more layers beneath. Like a very old, tattooed onion, she thought.

The hallway led to a huge, gloomy lobby lit only by the streaks of sunlight that could sneak through the cracks in the boarded windows. Ragged furniture and splintered wooden crates were scattered around the room on the dusty floor. When her eyes finally adjusted, Camden saw at least ten kids of her own age sitting quietly in a circle. Camden thought it was very peculiar that she hadn't heard a sound to let her know there was a whole gang of kids here. So this must be Mitch's new crowd, she thought. They're not very rowdy.

But as she and Mitch picked their way through the trash and broken lamps, she saw someone she knew.

"Hey, that's Dan Legeman . . . and Nancy Colletti! Mitch, we know these guys!" Camden was beginning to doubt his sanity.

"Never said we didn't," he answered and sat down on an old crate. Camden was left standing alone, feeling a little stupid.

"Uh, hi, Nancy," she stammered in an attempt to break the uncomfortable silence. Nancy Colletti was famous for her tan. She was usually a very deep brown by this time of year. But even in the dusty light, Camden could see that she was nowhere near as tan as she had been the previous summer. Nancy waved a limp greeting.

Tall, skinny Dan Legeman was sitting scrunched up on a low stool. Camden and Danny had known each other since the fourth grade, when he asked her to go steady with him. Camden had been bending over, stirring a pot of poster paint, when he came up and asked her to go steady. Even then, she hadn't thought it was a very good way to ask someone. They went together for a long time, but they never kissed or anything. In fact, they hardly ever talked or did things together. And at the end of a year, she gave him his Saint Christopher medal back. But secretly Camden knew Danny still liked her. When she saw him sitting in the hotel lobby, she thought he would at least smile at her. He hardly seemed to notice.

Nobody said a word. It was like the instant quiet of a classroom when the teacher turns off the lights. Camden tried to continue her conversation with Nancy.

"So, Nance. Where's your famous tan? Don't you guys ever go outside? I'm tanner than you and I've been in the mountains for a whole month!"

But Nancy just looked at her blankly and shrugged.

Fine, Camden thought. Forget it.

There was more silence. Finally, a girl Camden didn't know very well, named Sara Kleinman, spoke up.

"My grownies tried to stick me in prison-class all summer."

"Slimy grownies," Dan responded with disgust.

Camden stared at Sara, shocked.

"You mean your grandparents actually wanted to have you locked up in jail? I can't believe it!" she exclaimed.

Sara looked at Camden as if she were some sort of weird alien who couldn't understand the language. The others laughed and poked one another.

"No," Mitch whispered. "SK-2's grownies, uh . . . I mean, parents, tried to make her go to summer school."

"Oh!" she whispered back to him. "It sounded to me just like she said *prison*! My mistake!"

Camden was getting sarcastic because she was confused and beginning to think they were all against her.

Suddenly the sound of footsteps pounded above them on the second floor. All eyes turned up to follow the sound of the steps as they progressed down one side of the floor above, across, then down the other.

"Kidsters."

A calm voice came from the top of the grand lobby staircase and Camden looked up to see a shadowy figure leaning casually against the banister.

This must be WT-what's-his-name, she said to herself.

He walked slowly down the stairs and stopped at the bottom, one foot cocked on the last step, hand on hip.

"Now this is serious coolness," Camden muttered to Mitch under her breath. But he ignored her, his eyes riveted on the young man at the bottom of the stairs. Finally getting a good look at this WT-whatever guy, Camden wondered what the big deal was. He looked like any regular teenager in his perfectly faded jeans, his black "Space Invaders" T-shirt, nicely scuffed boots, and what looked like a genuine Dodgers baseball jacket. Camden figured him to be about fourteen or fifteen, but she couldn't tell exactly because his face was shaded by the large brim of a baseball cap.

As he proceeded toward the center of the group, Camden noticed that the best of the crummy chairs stood a little apart from the others, which were grouped in a semicircle around it.

WT nodded to each person. One by one they stepped back as he went by, as if they were in absolute awe of him.

Camden thought the whole thing was a little silly. WT reached his chair and turned toward them.

What are we all supposed to do, stand up and bow or what? she wondered.

"WT-3," Dan Legeman said, greeting him formally.

"DL-2," he answered with a nod.

"WT-3," Hank Matthews said.

"HM-1," he answered in return and went on around the group until he reached Mitch and Camden.

"WT-3," Mitch repeated, just as the others had done.

"MM-3." He nodded and turned to look Camden straight in the eye.

She disliked him instantly. There was something strange in his stare. She got the feeling that he was sizing her up, lurking, waiting for an opening, a weak spot. She broke the stare and looked away.

Mitch cleared his throat nervously.

"Uh, WT-3, the new Kidster's grownie name is Camden."

Grownie name? What does that mean? she wondered.

Camden finally looked back at WT.

"Nice to meet you," she said politely.

"Double good," he answered and sat down in his ragged chair.

Mitch shifted uncomfortably and pulled Camden down onto an old crate next to him.

"Am I embarrassing you, Mitch?" she whispered to him with irritation. But he just shook his head and stared at WT-3.

"Kidsters," he began, as if he were giving a speech. "It's

time to say double-bye to the rusty, dusty grownies with their drudge work and brain-drain of the prison schools. Time to forget their fogy rules. Time to do The Words!"

The kids sent up a cheer. Camden had absolutely no idea what he was talking about. It was weird but kind of interesting.

"Double good!" Mark Nieto said.

"The Words are vast, truly vast," Nancy agreed.

"Trash grownie thought!" Hank yelled.

"Kidsters," WT continued in a calm, controlled tone, "the grownies want us to buckle, to muddle-fuddle our minds with their meanings and rules and syllables and look-it-ups. But it's a no-go! We do The Words. They're too vast, too quick and clean for the grownies' vacuum-packed brains. Don't be a victim of grownie thinking. Do The Game to clear your minds of their thoughts and rules and words!"

At the mention of a game, the kids seemed to get very excited. They grinned and nudged each other eagerly, and Camden got the impression that something was finally going to happen.

At last, she thought. Now maybe we can get out of this dump! Her nose was beginning to itch and tickle from all the dust.

As the kids cheered him on, WT reached inside the pocket of his baseball jacket and brought out a small, dark something. Camden couldn't tell what it was exactly, but it seemed to be a kind of dull gray cube that fit in the palm of his hand.

This is what everybody's so excited about? she thought. Camden glanced over at Mitch, who was staring at that gray thing with a sort of half-smile on his face. It was a little like the way she'd seen him look at his big brother's Trans Am, kind of adoring.

Okay, she thought. This had better be good.

But then Camden felt a rough hand shove her out of the way as Hank Matthews shouldered past her toward WT-3. Hank had always been one of Camden's most *un*favorite people, ever since the time he'd stopped her on the way home from the grocery store. Hank had grabbed the bag out of her hands, taken the chips, and dumped the rest of it all over the ground. Not completely satisfied with that, he'd stomped on her mother's milk and eggs.

Camden had punched him, a good one right in the stomach that knocked all of his wind out. She knew it wasn't the right thing to do and her mom had even made her apologize. But Camden knew that Hank had never forgiven her and was just waiting for a chance to get even.

Glaring in Camden's direction, Hank spoke to WT with a sneer in his voice.

"She can't do The Game," he said. "She's no Kidster!"

WT turned to Hank with a cool, soothing smile.

"HM-1, you were un-Kidster once yourself. Don't be greedy; that's grownie thinking."

Grumbling, Hank returned to his place as the Kidsters formed a circle around WT. Camden stood next to Mitch, not quite sure what she was supposed to do.

Standing very still in the middle of the group, WT held

the gray cube thing in the palm of his hand while the others began to chant.

"The Game, The Game, The Game," they repeated over and over.

Mitch nudged Camden to join in, but she felt too stupid. Very slowly, the Kidsters began to circle WT-3. Chanting louder now, they turned around him faster and faster. Camden was swept along with them, but she tried to keep an eye on WT. He kept staring at the gray cube and she could see lines of concentration crisscross his forehead. It was as if he were pouring all of his energy into that little gray cube. Just for a second, Camden thought she could see tiny sparks shoot out from his eyes.

The circle began to pick up more speed, forcing Camden to take her eyes off WT so she could keep her balance. There was a steady rhythm to the chanting that seemed to beat inside her head. When she was able to look back at him, Camden was sure she could see bright sparks shooting out of WT's eyes toward the cube.

Then it began to move. The cube twirled slowly as if the chanting and the circle and WT's effort had brought it to life. Suddenly it twisted around and up. Standing upright on one corner, the cube spun at an incredible speed. Camden's jaw dropped open.

As it spun, the color began to darken from a dull gray into a deep blackness that seemed to go on and on forever inside that cube. Camden felt as if she were looking into a deep emptiness, a void that seemed to draw her inside itself. She lost all sense of where she was as she felt herself slipping away, swallowed up by that spinning vortex.

The feeling was both pleasant and unpleasant at the same time. But she knew for sure that whatever was pulling her in was very much stronger than she. Camden tried to take a step forward, but her legs were like long, wobbly noodles and she felt herself falling forward toward the floor. She seemed to fall for a very long time and she was afraid she was going to bang her head when she finally landed. But somehow the floor had changed. It was soft when she landed, like a huge white pillow that bounced her right back up again.

"Mitch," she called, and her voice seemed to come from very far away. It seemed to echo down a long tunnel and disappear like a train speeding away into the distance. Camden tried to say something else, but she couldn't exactly put the words together right. Her thoughts wandered aimlessly through her head and, somehow, whatever she wanted to say kept slipping out of her grasp.

Suddenly Camden saw a huge bird flapping toward her. She ducked her head just in time as the bird hit the wall and bounced off again. Only it wasn't a bird. It was Mitch. He bounced past her, giggling wildly, and soon Camden began to notice the rest of her friends. They were all leaping up and falling on the floor, bouncing off, hitting the wall, and bouncing away again. They all looked so funny she began to giggle, too. She couldn't help herself. She laughed so hard she fell that long way to the floor again and she bounced up and back past her hysterical friends. Camden felt like a runaway Ping-Pong ball, bouncing and landing and bouncing away again.

But when she landed the last time, the floor seemed to engulf her in its pillowy softness. She tried to stand up, but her feet kept slipping deep into the soft folds, and she fell backward into the white marshmallow floor. It wrapped itself around her as a thick drowsiness stole her away into a heavy sleep.

Camden awoke to an unpleasant itching in her nose. She brushed at her face, then opened her eyes. She was lying face down on the grimy floor of the abandoned hotel lobby. She scratched at the dust in her nose again and sat up, bleary-eyed. The rest of the kids were scattered around the floor in jumbled heaps as if they had all fallen down in a game of Crack-the-Whip.

When she was finally able to speak, Camden's voice was dry and scratchy.

"Wow," she croaked. "That was some game!"

The others began to stir as Camden moved over to Mitch, who was lying across a ragged chair. She poked him with her foot.

"Mitch, did that really happen? What did he do with that cube thing? I can't believe it! I was bouncing all over the room!"

He sat up, rubbing his eyes, and grinned at her.

"Pretty good, huh?" he said in a raspy voice.

By this time the Kidsters had gathered in a group and were chattering happily.

"Mondo-cosmic or what?"

"That was limboland! Did you see me come zooming off the wall?"

"You almost trashed SK-2!"

"That was the absolute double best so far!"

Camden and Mitch joined them and she started asking questions as fast as she could think of them.

"How did he *do* that?" she demanded. "That had to be the most bizarre thing that's ever happened to me! What was that cube thing?"

They stopped talking and looked at her scornfully.

"The power-unit," Mitch mumbled in answer to her last question.

"Power-unit?" she repeated. "Where did he get it? How does it work?"

But no one answered her as they started gathering their stuff to go home.

"You guys!" Camden protested loudly. "I can't believe you're all acting as if this weird cube thing happens every day!"

"It does," Mitch told her. "It's The Game."

She sighed. "I know it's a game. But how did he do it?" She glanced around for WT-3. "Where did he go, anyway?"

"Behind the door-unit," Mark answered.

Camden scratched her head in confusion.

"Door-unit? Power-unit? What is this with everything-unit?"

"It's The Words." Mitch pulled at her arm. "Lezgo, Camden."

But she was not about to be put off so easily.

"Wait, I just want to find out where this door-unit thing is so I can ask him what —"

Hank interrupted her rudely.

"WT says asking questions is grownie thinking. Besides, only *he's* allowed behind the door-unit."

"I just want to ask him where he got that cube . . . power-unit thing," she continued quickly. "Just tell me where he is and . . ."

Ignoring her, they filed out of the lobby. Camden trailed behind them, firing questions fast and furious.

Camden had to squint against the bright sunlight as they emerged from the gloomy building. Confused and very frustrated, Camden leaned against the stucco wall. She could feel a headache coming on. After the others had ridden away on bikes and skateboards, she turned to Mitch with an angry glare.

"C'mon, Mitch!" she begged. "Are you going to tell me what's going on here or not? That was a pretty strange thing that happened in there and I'm feeling kind of funny about it."

He smiled. "You did good, Camden. Lezgo to the pier."

"Will you tell me then?" she asked.

But he was already pedaling down the block.

"Fine!" she grumbled and grabbed her bike to follow him.

As usual the boardwalk was a mass of people walking, running, or roller-skating. So Mitch and Camden were forced to walk their bikes on the boardwalk as they shuffled along in the sand.

"So what was that power thing, Mitch?" she asked for the umpteenth time. "Is it some new kind of video game or something?"

"No," he answered. "WT-3 uses the power-unit to make The Game."

"Well, were we hypnotized or something?" she asked.

He thought for a minute. "Hypnotized?"

"Yeah," she answered. "You know, like . . ." She used her deepest voice. "You're falling into a deep, deeeep, sleeeeeep . . ."

"No, I don't think so," he said. "But what difference does it make? You had fun, didn't you?"

"Well, yeah, but . . ." She frowned. "But don't you think we should know what this WT guy is doing to us? I mean, what if it's drugs or something?"

"It's not drugs, Camden," he assured her. "WT says it's the power of our own minds. There's nothing wrong with that, is there?"

She shook her head.

"I don't know, Mitch."

Sand was creeping into Camden's tennis shoes. She stopped to scratch her ankles. Mitch didn't seem to care about itchy ankles.

"The grownies try to keep us from using our minds. They are always trying to make us think their double ungood grownie thoughts and —"

Camden held up her hands.

"Wait! Wait a second! Now what is this language? I felt like an idiot because I didn't understand what anybody was saying!"

"The Words are for us, for Kidsters," he explained.

She considered his statement.

"You mean, these words —"

"The Words," he corrected her.

"The Words are some sort of secret language that only kids know?" That sounded kind of fun.

"WT-3 speaks The Words," he went on. "Only Kidsters who hang with him can speak The Words."

"So he's teaching everybody a secret language, like a code that only kids are allowed to learn, right?" she asked.

He nodded. "Only Kidsters with The Words belong."

"Then it's a way for kids to talk together without adults knowing what they're saying." Camden liked this more and more.

"Right," he answered.

"So we could be talking in front of our parents —" she continued.

"Grownies," he corrected her.

"Grownies?" She giggled.

"Grownies are all adults," he explained.

"Okay," she said. "So we could say anything we wanted and not one grownie would get it!"

He smiled at her.

"Pretty cosmic, huh?"

"Yeah." She giggled again. "I could tell you that my

mom's lasagna tastes like wax paper and she would never know what I said!" They both laughed at the thought. Mitch was very familiar with her mother's cooking.

"Double right," he said.

The sight of the Santa Monica pier made Camden's stomach growl.

"Hey, Mitch. Let's go get some *real* potato chips at that fish place on the pier." This particular fish-and-chips stand made its chips with slices of real potato, skin and all.

Later, munching on chips and dangling their feet off the edge of the pier, Camden asked Mitch why the other kids had been so unfriendly.

"You're not a Kidster, Camden," he explained. "You don't even have a Kidster code."

"You mean, those initials that WT-what's-his-name kept calling everyone? What's wrong with their real names?" she asked.

He snorted. "No need for names. Names are grownie talk."

"Oh," she said. "So this WT, HM, PJ stuff is a secret code. The person's initials, right? But what's the number part?"

He looked confused. "The number?"

"Yeah, like HM-1, DL-2, like that. What does the number stand for?" she asked.

"The number," he repeated. He looked as if he had no idea what she meant.

"Mitch, the *number*," she said impatiently. "Like one, two . . ."

"Oh!" he said finally. "That's how many brothers and sisters the Kidster has."

She looked at him for a moment, then nodded her head.

"I see," she said. "So you're MM-3 because you've got two big brothers."

"Double ungood grownie brothers," he answered, frowning.

That's strange, Camden thought. He always liked his big brothers before.

She figured out her own Kidster title. "And I'd be CD-1 because I've got only me."

He nodded.

She liked the sound of it. "CD-1. It sounds so science fiction."

Mitch frowned again. "What?"

"Science fiction," she said again.

"Science fiction?" he repeated.

She was getting tired of this.

"Yes, Mitch! Science fiction!" She stared at him. "C'mon, you're the big sci-fi expert, not me!"

He stood up abruptly.

"So you want to speak The Words or no?" he asked.

"Sure."

She threw some chips to a sea gull to see if he could catch them in midair.

"It'd be fun, I guess. But I gotta tell you now, I'm not crazy about that WT guy."

On the fourth try, the gull snagged a chip.

"You will be," he answered smugly.

Camden finished off the chips and crumpled the bag.

"I doubt it."

She walked over to a nearby trash can to throw away the bag, and when she turned around, Mitch was gone.

What is the matter with him? she asked herself. Then she quickly grabbed her bike and rode after her best friend, swerving to avoid the crowd on the pier.

4

Busted

THAT EVENING Camden helped her mother make a chocolate soufflé. The rest of the dinner was take-out.

"Mom, I think you're supposed to whip those egg whites more." She looked in the cookbook. "It says here that they should stand up in peaks."

"Well, that's just fine," her mom answered, whipping furiously. "But my arm will never last until peaks."

"I'll take over for a while," Camden volunteered.

"Nope, I'm the mother here. I'm supposed to be able to do this kind of thing." She whipped faster. "So tell me what you did today. It'll keep my mind off the pain."

"Well," Camden answered, "Mitch and I want to see this new friend of his who has a very weird name and there was this new bunch of kids, but they weren't really new because I already knew them all."

For some reason, she didn't want to tell her mom about the gray cube or what had happened when she looked into it.

"Oh," her mom answered, whipping with vigor. "So who is this new friend with the weird name?"

"Oh, just some guy that everybody thinks is totally hip," Camden told her.

"Everybody?" Her mother raised an eyebrow.

Camden groaned. Why don't parents ever let kids get away with anything? she wondered.

"No, Mom, not *everybody*," she said, casting her eyes heavenward.

Her mother stared at the foamy egg whites.

"Is this the peaks?" she asked. "I still don't see any peaks."

Camden urged her on.

"Keep going, Mom. You just haven't whipped them hard enough."

Mrs. Douglas pressed her lips together tightly and bent to the task.

"So where does this new 'hip' guy live?" she asked.

Camden answered without thinking.

"Venice," she said and froze.

The word hung awkwardly in the air, making Camden wish she could take it back. The whipping stopped.

"You went to Venice without asking permission?"

Camden could hear the surprise verging on anger in her mother's voice. She had completely forgotten about the whole thing and now she was busted. Her only hope was to divert her attention and stall for time.

"Don't stop whipping, Mom! You'll ruin it!" she exclaimed.

Mrs. Douglas weighed the importance of her soufflé against the magnitude of Camden's crime. She started whipping again, slowly.

Camden thought fast. She decided that the best approach at this point was total honesty.

"I'm sorry, Mom. I didn't know we were going there before you left this morning. And I didn't call because I . . ." She shrugged. "I just forgot."

Camden listened to the sound of the wire whisk hitting the side of the bowl faster and faster. Her mother cleared her throat.

"You forgot?"

"Yes, Mom," she answered, trying to look as innocent as possible. "I throw myself on the mercy of the court."

"All right, Camden." Mrs. Douglas was using her Teacher Voice. "Just go to your room until dinner."

Camden twisted a button on her shirt.

"Are you going to tell Dad?" she asked quietly.

"I don't know," her mother answered, still using her Teacher Voice. "Just go to your room."

Camden stood there for a few more seconds, then slipped quickly out of the kitchen. On her way up the stairs, she could hear the sound of egg whites being whipped to death.

It is difficult to hold your breath and eat dinner at the same time. Camden nearly choked that night trying it. She held her breath, waiting fearfully for her mother to tell her dad about that illegal trip to Venice. But her mother was merciful and they made it through the whole meal without a mention of it. Camden returned the favor when dessert was served.

Mr. Douglas stared at the flat brown blob lying in the soufflé dish.

"What's this?" he asked delicately.

Mrs. Douglas heaved a sigh.

"Well, it was supposed to be a —"

"A giant brownie, Dad!" Camden interrupted quickly and gave her mom a wink.

"Oh?" He peered at the deflated soufflé. "I've never seen such a big one!"

Camden's mother smiled at her with gratitude. Leaning over to cut the "brownie," she whispered, "We're even."

5

A Star Wind Sweeps Her Up

FLOATING, FLOATING. Camden was floating free above her bed, gently gliding, softly drifting. Suddenly, without warning, she began to fall through a long, dark tunnel. Down she fell, faster and faster, and she couldn't stop. Then a brisk wind came out of nowhere and caught her up. She was bounced up and whipped smoothly over and around, like a wild roller coaster ride. Only it was all roller and no coaster.

Camden loved to dream. She pretended her dreams were wonderful, scary adventures in which anything could happen. She even liked nightmares, the scarier the better. Whenever she got too afraid, there was a small inner voice that told her the dream wasn't real. Then she knew that she could always wake up if it got too bad.

This was a good dream. She was flying into a vast, black void. But soon she was surrounded by stars, winking and blinking all around her. The wind grew stronger. It whipped and twirled her over and up and through space. She was riding on a wild night wind, speeding past the stars. All she could see was a deep, velvet darkness lit by dazzling, sparkling lights going on and on without end. She felt as if she could ride this Star Wind into forever, and it was so wonderful that she forgot to be afraid.

Way off in the distance, Camden began to see a large glowing ball, bigger and brighter than the twinkling stars. As it grew closer, she marveled at the brilliant light that streaked the blackness with gleaming sunbeams. This alien sun showered a deep golden-bronze glow onto a very small planet that lay beneath it.

As she twirled toward the bronze planet, Camden realized that this must be where her dream was taking her. She spiraled down through warm, golden skies in which small white clouds whizzed past. Before long, she found herself falling gently down toward a lovely bronze city. She floated down past the high windows of skyscrapers, past a lovely park with golden leaves that were beginning to fall from bronze branches, and softly down onto a busy sidewalk.

Camden looked around at the people hurrying by and she felt disappointed.

"This is no fun!" she complained to her dream. "It's exactly like Earth and the people look exactly like the people at home. I was expecting something a little more exciting."

Just then Camden noticed a young woman stop to look at herself in a store window. When the girl pulled off her hat, beautiful hair tumbled to her shoulders. Camden had never seen hair that color before. It glowed with the same bronze shine that came from the glorious sun.

"Wow," Camden mumbled, "bronze hair!"

Then she looked closer at the other people on the busy street. She noticed a bronze-headed boy riding his bike through the crowd. She saw a businessman with bronze hair in a three-piece suit. She spotted an entire family with bronze locks and even an old woman whose gray hair peeked out from under a short bronze wig.

"Everybody's got bronze hair!" Camden exclaimed. "I guess they don't look *exactly* like the people at home."

Then she noticed that as normal as this city appeared to be, she had not yet heard a single sound. It seemed as if she were watching a silent movie.

Mmmmmmm, she thought.

Without warning, the dream picked her up again and glided her down the street about three feet above the sidewalk.

"Hey!" she laughed. "This just might be fun after all."

Soon Camden found herself in front of a huge black glass building that somehow seemed out of place in the warm, welcoming bronze city. She glided up the large steps and read the words GREAT HALL OF LEARNING written over the huge black glass doors.

Hall of Learning? she thought. I wonder what that is.

As if in answer, the dream whisked her right through the doors.

"Fantastic," she exclaimed. "I can glide through doors!"

She entered a long hallway in which lots of people were lined up behind rows of doors that had strange names on them like ADJECTIVE INVESTIGATION, PREPOSITIONAL PHRASE FOUNDATION, and BUREAU OF THE NOUN AND PRONOUN.

This is a truly weird dream, Camden thought as she came to the end of the hall and another huge glass door. GRAND CLASSROOM, she read, and glided right through without a pause.

Inside the Grand Classroom, Camden was hit by an incredible clamor. It was as if her dream's soundtrack had suddenly kicked in at top volume. The room was full of people talking, scraping chairs, and yelling across the room until they were silenced by the loud *Whap! Whap! Whap!* of a judge's gavel.

Camden had never been in a courtroom before, but she had seen lots of them on television. This was definitely a courtroom, no matter what it said on the door. The audience sat in one area behind a little gate. There was a place for defendants, a jury box, and even a judge's bench.

But the judge's bench in the dream was shaped exactly like a large teacher's desk. There were papers strewn about, lots of difficult-looking books piled high, and several red pencils jammed into a pencil holder.

And the judge sitting behind the desk looked remarkably like a teacher. She had dark bronze hair pulled into a bun at the back of her head, little silver spectacles perched on a pretty face. In place of judge's robes, she wore a nice respectable teacher's dress. Camden knew a teacher when she saw one.

In the jury box, a number of student types were busy polishing apples, sharpening pencils, or asking permission.

Must be teacher's pets, Camden thought.

There were also several people with dunce caps slumped

on tall stools in dark corners around the room.

Whap! Whap! Whap! The Teacher banged for silence once again, and Camden noticed that her gavel was a huge Golden Ruler.

"Class! Find a seat!" she thundered in a voice that sounded like a slap across the face. Camden would never have imagined such a voice coming from so pretty a lady.

Well, I was wrong about this one, she thought. She's a total witch.

Camden moved closer to watch as the Teacher surveyed the room, daring anyone to disobey. When the Teacher's gaze swept past Camden, she felt a chill streak right past the safety of the dream and into her heart. It was the exact same feeling that she got when she looked into the rattle-snake's eyes behind the thick glass at the zoo — cold, un-caring, deadly. It frightened her so much that she almost decided to wake up.

Wait a sec, she said to herself. This is one of the best dreams you've ever had. Don't blow it now.

The crowd quieted obediently and the Teacher cleared her throat.

"Stand! The first defendant!" she bellowed.

A very nervous gentleman, seated in a little child's desk much too small for him, tried to untangle himself and stand up. He squeezed and struggled while the Pets giggled; finally he managed to escape. But he still looked a bit folded as he stood before the Teacher, his poor hat a crumpled ball in his hands.

The Teacher spoke soothingly with that kind of sickly

sweet tone that adults often use with a naughty child.

"You know that walking your dog without a leash is illegal, now don't you?" she asked, glaring down at him over her spectacles.

"Yes, your ma'amship." His voice trembled and he couldn't seem to keep his hands from his pathetic hat. "But you see, I had misplaced the leash and . . . the dog had to—" His face reddened. "Had to . . . uh . . . go, you see, so I thought this once—"

The Teacher snorted. "Well! How would it be if we all did things we shouldn't just because we didn't take the time to follow the rules? Hmmmmm?" She peered at him.

The Pets stopped their busywork to listen while the little gentleman twitched and tore at his hat.

"I . . . guess it'd be a mess, ma'am."

She laughed too loudly. "A fine mess!"

"But the dog had to go." His voice shook.

"No excuses!" she screamed.

Whap! went the Golden Ruler.

"I sentence you to one hundred story problems due tomorrow morning!"

The people in the audience sucked in their breath and the gentleman's mouth flew open.

"One hundred?" he stammered in disbelief.

"Eight A.M.!" she answered and smiled at the Pets.

"But—but—" the little gentleman protested, "that's not fair! I can't do one hundred story problems by tomorrow morning."

The Teacher tried to look as though she cared.

"Oh, dear!" she cooed in her sickly sweet voice. "Isn't that just awful. Tut, tut."

The Teacher's Pets nodded and aahed and shook their heads in mock sympathy. The Teacher smiled.

"So I'll make it . . . *two hundred*," she thundered at him, "because I don't like your attitude! Next case!" she bellowed.

Slam went the Golden Ruler. The defeated man with the crumpled brown rag could do nothing but stumble out of the Grand Classroom while the Teacher's Pets giggled and pointed at him scornfully.

But the rest of the audience was not pleased. They grumbled among themselves and the grumbling turned to a small *Boo*, which built to a large *Boo!* that was met by the *Whap-Whap-Whapping!* The noise grew and grew until Camden couldn't stand it anymore. She covered her ears, and when that didn't help, she woke herself up.

Camden lay very still in her bed for a moment, surprised by the sudden quiet.

"Whew!" She turned over and almost squashed her sleeping cat.

"Maggie, you wouldn't believe the dream I just had. Too bizarre!"

Maggie purred politely and stretched out one paw, but she didn't seem to care.

"Maggie, wake up!" Camden poked her. "I have to tell you about this dream!"

"Maw," she answered sleepily and rolled over so Camden

could scratch her tummy. Scratching, Camden told Maggie about the dream.

"Is that ultra-strange or what?" she asked her purring cat.

Maggie thought it was.

"And that poor little man, all those Teacher's Pets laughing at him. I would have told them off!"

Camden sat up straight. Suddenly she had remembered the events of that afternoon.

"Oh, Maggie, I forgot to tell you! The weirdest thing happened today! Mitch and I went to this decrepit hotel and there was this strange kid named WT-3 and he did something with this tiny gray cube! We were bouncing all over the room like Ping-Pong balls!"

Maggie twitched an ear back. She knew Camden liked to exaggerate just a little.

"Really!" Camden continued. "You should have been there! I couldn't believe it! And they're all talking a strange language that only kids are supposed to understand."

Maggie studied Camden seriously. She thought the whole situation sounded very odd. Maybe Camden shouldn't go back there.

"Well . . ." Camden answered. "The Game was really fun. Mitch doesn't think there's anything wrong with it. And this secret language sounds like a kick. Besides, I'm going to feel pretty stupid if I'm the only one who doesn't know it."

Maggie agreed that the secret language might be interesting. But she didn't like the sound of that WT person or bouncing all over the room like a Ping-Pong ball. She yawned so broadly that Camden could see all of her little sharp teeth.

"Okay," she said. "Go back to sleep. I can take a hint."

Maggie purred and curled up, tucking her head under a paw. She was instantly asleep.

Camden leaned over to her bedside table and picked up *The Jungle Books*. In moments she was completely absorbed in the story of Mowgli the wolf boy and his fight with the terrible tiger, her dream almost forgotten.

6

Everybody's Mad

THE NEXT MORNING, after doing all the chores on her mom's list, Camden called her friend.

"Mitch! I have to return some books to the library. Wanna come? We could get some more, then go play video games. Sound like a plan?"

"Kidster," he answered flatly, "thought you wanted to speak The Words."

"I do," she said. "What's that got to do with the library and video games?"

"Got to go to WT-3's," he said impatiently.

"Again?" she asked.

"Only way to learn," he replied.

Oh boy, Camden thought to herself, he is really into this thing.

"Mitch, I can't go to Venice again," she explained. "My mom's still mad about yesterday. I just barely escaped very deep trouble last night."

"So leave her a note," he answered. "Tell her we went to a movie."

"I can't do that!" she exclaimed.

There was a long silence. Camden thought he'd hung up.

"Mitch? Are you there?" she said into the phone.

"Thought you wanted to hang with us and WT-3," he answered softly.

Camden didn't like the sound of that.

"Oh, I see! You're going there anyway, with or without me, right?"

Mitch and Camden always did things together — *always*. They were best friends, after all.

"Come with, Camden," he pleaded, sounding a little more like his old self. "Just leave a note. We'll speak The Words and stuff . . ."

She gave in. "Oh, all right, Mitch. If it's such a big deal. I guess my mom will never know the difference."

Besides, she really wanted to have another go at that game. Mitch breathed a sigh of relief.

"Great! Mine in ten!" he said, hanging up.

"Boy oh boy," Camden mumbled to herself. "The things I do for a friend."

She scrawled a quick note, trying to ignore the guilt she was already feeling. She knew other kids lied to their parents a lot, but she had never really needed to.

I guess they trust me, she thought.

Before she could change her mind, Camden slammed the note under the magnet on the refrigerator and turned to leave. But Maggie dashed in front of her, sitting down right smack in front of the door. Camden stopped, her escape blocked. She put her hands on her hips and glared at her cat.

"Now what? I suppose you want to go too?"

Maggie looked up at her with those deep blue eyes until Camden gave in.

"Oh, all right." She sighed. "You can come. I can't deal with any more problems today."

She laid her backpack on the floor and Maggie stepped neatly inside to curl up in the bottom. Camden hoisted the pack onto her back. Then she grabbed her bike and they were off, Maggie's little cat head peering over the edge of the bag.

Unfortunately, Mitch was not at all pleased to see Maggie. There was the usual trouble with the dogs at the door. While he was struggling with them, he told her that the cat should stay home.

"Aw, c'mon, Mitch! My mom's already mad. If I leave Maggie, *she*'ll be mad, and now *you're* mad!" She threw up her hands. "It's too much! Why don't we just forget the whole thing!"

"Okay, okay," he answered quickly. "She comes but WT won't like it."

"What are you talking about?" Camden demanded, coming to her cat's defense. "Everybody likes Maggie."

"Believe it. He won't," Mitch answered. "My droolers aren't allowed."

He threw the last dog through the door and slammed it shut.

"Lezgo!"

Riding down to Venice, Camden took deep breaths of the salty air and watched the emerald-green ocean heave and surge against the white shore. She yelled across to Mitch as they rode together.

"Hey! Guess what book I was reading at camp!"

"Don't know," he answered without much interest.

"No, guess!" she called. "I'll give you a hint. It has to do with a man-cub and his gray brothers."

Mitch shrugged and pulled ahead of her a little. She pedaled faster to keep up.

"Come on, Mitch! It's easy!" she yelled over at him. "I'll give you another hint. We both read it in fourth grade!"

Ignoring her, he pedaled faster and pulled ahead again. Frowning, Camden speeded up.

"Mitch! I can't believe you aren't getting this. Remember Baloo and Kaa and —"

Mitch moved ahead and really put some distance between them. Camden pedaled furiously but she couldn't catch up.

"Mitch, wait up!" she yelled after him. But he didn't even slow down.

"Well," she muttered, "I take it he doesn't want to know the name of the book."

"Maw," Maggie answered from deep within the backpack.

7

Soda Pop

CAMDEN HAD a little trouble finding the side street, but she and Maggie finally arrived at the old, falling-down (Something) View Arms. Mitch was waiting.

"Mitch! What is your story?" she demanded, trying to make her bike lean against the building. "Why did you ride off like that?" She couldn't get the right angle to make the bike stay up.

He shrugged. "Wanted to get here double quick."

"Well, it wasn't very nice," she told him.

Just then, Dan Legeman and Marvin Washington screeched around the corner and leaped off their bikes.

"Kidsters!" they called in greeting as they ran down the side of the hotel and disappeared down the steps. Mitch followed them without waiting for Camden. She hurriedly pushed her bike against the wall and rushed after them. She didn't want to get left behind in that scary old basement again. As she squeezed through the door, Camden heard her bike crash to the ground.

She managed to keep Maggie in the backpack until she

reached the hallway with the peeling wallpaper. But that was as long as she could stand it, because sharp claws were pricking her shoulder.

"Ow! Maggie! Okay, I'll let you down. Just get your claws out of my neck!"

Maggie leaped to the floor and sniffed the air for a moment, then pranced away to explore, tail held high.

Camden and Mitch found their friends camped around the murky lobby again, and they sat down to wait for WT-3.

"Are we going to play The Game again?" Camden asked eagerly. A few Kidsters nodded in reply. Camden felt a little tickle of excitement in the pit of her stomach and looked up with anticipation when she heard the familiar footsteps on the floor above them.

But at the exact moment WT-3 appeared at the top of the stairs, Maggie trotted up from the other direction. They surprised each other. Maggie skidded to a halt, back arched, ears flat, her tail a bottle brush. She growled deep in her throat, hissing a warning.

WT gave a frightened yelp and almost fell down the steps. He grabbed at the railing and held on, gasping for breath.

Camden thought that was one of the funniest things she'd ever seen. She laughed so hard at the sight of them scaring each other that she almost fell over onto the floor. But she quickly realized that she was the only one in hysterics. The Kidsters, even Mitch, glared at her with disapproval, and her giggles died in her throat.

WT was furious. He stomped down the stairs in a huff, adjusting his baseball cap.

"No mewlers!" he yelled angrily.

Maggie had disappeared somewhere and was probably looking down at them from the rafters, snickering to herself. When Mitch shot Camden a disapproving "I-told-you-so" look, she stood up.

"Maggie, let's get out of here!" she called. "We know when we're not wanted!"

"Kidster." WT's voice was calm and soothing. The anger was gone. "It's okay about the mewler. You didn't know." He cast a cold glare at Mitch.

"I *knew* that cats aren't allowed," she told him in a belligerent tone. "Mitch told me, so don't get on his case. But, see, Maggie's not just any old cat."

WT cocked an eyebrow. "You knew?" he asked.

"Sure," she replied. "But I think it's a stupid rule and —"

WT chuckled. He seemed to be enjoying this little challenge. His voice became velvet.

"Kidster, we want you to hang with us." He turned to the group. "Don't we?"

They nodded and almost looked as though they meant it.

"But if you want to stay and learn The Words," he went on, "you have to start acting like a Kidster, and Kidsters don't deal with mewlers."

"Well," Camden answered him, "she's my cat and I'll deal with her whenever I feel like it. But she probably won't want to come back here anyway after you scared her to death!"

He studied Camden for a moment before nodding slowly. "Double good."

The Game was different this time. It started out exactly as it had before, with the Kidsters circling WT and his spinning power-unit. Camden eagerly joined in the chant as the group moved faster and faster. She saw those same bright sparks flash from WT's eyes and she felt that incredible force pulling her deeper and deeper into the empty black void. Then everything went topsy-turvy.

The whole room seemed to rock sideways at a funny angle and Camden found herself standing all alone in the middle of an immense brown desert. She looked around for signs of her friends, but all she could see was miles and miles of flat ground with a few gray boulders scattered here and there. There wasn't a tree or a cactus or even a lizard to keep her company.

"This isn't like the other time," she said aloud, but her voice sounded small and frightened.

Camden wondered if maybe this was all just a dream. But it didn't feel like one of her adventure dreams. She never got scared in them because there was always that tiny voice inside telling her everything was okay. There was no tiny voice this time. And none of this felt okay. There was something unnatural about it, wrong in some way.

Camden had the sudden urge to start screaming for Mitch, for her friends, even for WT-3. Anybody! She squeezed her fists together as tightly as she could to calm herself down.

"Get a grip, Camden," she scolded herself. "Don't push the panic button."

Her dad always said that. It made her feel better to think about him. She took ten deep breaths and tried to concentrate on what she should do. The most intelligent thing would be to walk in one direction until she ran into something she recognized. West; she'd head west toward the ocean.

Camden glanced up at the sky to get her bearings by the sun and she almost panicked again. The sun was gone. The only thing she could see up there was brownish sky. No sun, no clouds, no birds, no airplanes — nothing but a dusty emptiness. Camden bravely fought the urge to sit down and cry as she forced one foot in front of the other in the direction of what she hoped was the ocean.

She walked for a long time. She passed hundreds of oddly shaped rocks and boulders. Once she saw a large, flat metal disk that seemed to be made of copper. It was round with funny markings etched into the top and sides. Camden didn't go near it. She'd seen too many space-alien movies.

Farther on she passed a huge white thing that was as big as a house. But it didn't have any doors or windows and one end was kind of crushed down with some brownish, haylike stuff sticking out. She hurried past that one, too.

Hours later, Camden began to hear noises. She couldn't quite be sure, but it sounded like people yelling and laughing. Once she thought she heard a loud splash.

"The ocean!" she exclaimed and began to run. Soon, far

off in the distance, Camden spotted something very large, a kind of huge shiny cylinder. Her lungs ached but she kept running, desperate to find some human beings. Finally Camden saw them. They were surrounding that enormous cylinder. Some of the people were even on top of it. The cylinder was lying on one side and it appeared to be made out of tin or some kind of metal. There were huge pictures painted all over it and a keyholelike opening in one end. But the strangest thing was the lake that surrounded it. The gargantuan cylinder was sitting in the middle of an orange lake. As she grew closer, Camden realized that the people were her friends, the Kidsters. She threw back her head and yelled as loud as she could.

"You guys! Hey! You guys!"

Then she took off, running and tumbling toward her friends. Mitch was doing the backstroke across the shimmering orange lake when Camden arrived, panting, at the edge.

"Mitch! Hey, Mitch! Where are we?" she yelled across to him. He waved and kicked lazily toward her.

"CD-1, double good," he called.

"Where *are* we?" she repeated with a dry throat.

"Double don't know," he answered, splashing toward her.

"Mitch, I'm dying of thirst," she complained. "I've got to find some water."

"You can drink this stuff," he answered, climbing out of the lake onto the dry, flat desert floor.

Orange droplets fell from his wet trunks, forming puddles at his feet. She looked at it doubtfully.

"What if it's poison?" she asked.

"It's not poison, Camden," he scoffed. "It's sweet! I'm going back in. C'mon!"

She grabbed his arm. It was sticky.

"Mitch, where *are* we?" she asked for the third time.

"Who cares?"

He laughed and did a cannonball into the lake, splashing her with that orange, sticky stuff. She leaned down and scooped up a handful of it. She took a teensy sip.

"It *is* sweet!" she exclaimed, then gulped down another handful thirstily. "Well, if it's poison, I guess we'll know in a minute."

The answer hit Camden like a bolt out of the blue.

"Of course!" she cried, scooping up another handful of the colored liquid. She let it run through her fingers.

"Mitch!" she yelled across to him. "It's pop! Orange soda pop!"

Without warning, the strange world began to turn topsy-turvy again. That same heavy drowsiness overcame her like a curtain drawn across her eyes, and she was pulled down, down, into a deep sleep.

"Maw?"

Camden awoke to the silky touch of a cat's nose on her cheek.

"Maw?"

Maggie poked at her gently with a soft paw, and Camden blinked awake to find her cat's worried eyes peering into her own.

"Magg," she croaked. "How are ya?"

Camden shook her head to clear the web of sleep and felt a dull ache cross her forehead.

"Ahhh, my head," she moaned.

Maggie began pacing nervously back and forth in front of her. "Maw," she said again, insistent.

"Oh, Maggie, lighten up," Camden told her. "We'll leave in a little bit." She got to her feet, rubbing her temples. Mitch and the others were already awake and sharing their big adventure.

"Did you see me do that backward double loop into the orange water?" the super-athletic Mark asked them.

"Mondo-weird or what?" Danny said.

"*Beyond* the Twilight Zone!" Marvin answered.

"I know where we were!" Camden announced, joining them. "That was orange soda pop and the big cylinder was a pop can. Don't you see? We were shrunk! He shrunk us and we spent all that time right here in this room, super tiny! Can you believe it?"

They looked at her doubtfully.

"That's a no-go," Hank said, sneering. "We were out in the ozone somewhere."

Camden glanced around and picked up a shiny penny off the gritty floor.

"See!" She showed them the penny. "I saw this when I was walking through the desert. I thought it was some kind of spaceship or something. And this!"

She snatched up a cigarette butt from the floor.

"This cigarette butt! I thought it was an alien's house!"

Over their negative murmurs, Mitch called out from a corner of the room.

"She's right!"

He pointed to a half-empty soda can lying on its side in a pool of sticky orange pop. The Kidsters rushed over, gathering around it wide-eyed.

"Look at that!" Marvin mumbled. "We *were* shrunk!"

"Too extreme!" Nancy muttered.

"How did he do that?" Camden asked them. "I mean, that's impossible, isn't it?"

They glanced sharply at her.

"It's The Game," Danny answered with a stern look on his face.

Camden rubbed her temples again. The headache was worse.

"I know, I know it's 'The Game,'" she answered impatiently. "But aren't you guys just the tiniest bit curious about what he does with that . . . uh . . . power-unit?"

"That's a no-go, CD-1," Mark informed her. "WT says whys and whereofs and whatnots are double ungood grownie ways."

Mumbling to herself with frustration, Camden turned around just in time to see Hank deliver a swift kick at Maggie, who was waiting patiently for Camden on an empty crate. She hissed at him and leaped off in time to avoid the blow as Camden yelled and ran toward them.

"Hey!" She picked Maggie up protectively.

"WT says mewlers are a double badness," Hank snorted. "You'd better trash that one before he does."

"Listen, Hank Matthews," she answered angrily, "you'd just better trash your face because it's a triple ungood gross-out!"

That got a laugh from the other kids.

"Hey," Mitch said, laughing, "CD-1 speaks The Words!"

Hank squinted angry eyes at her and struggled to come up with a good insult to fling back at her. But Camden had outclassed him.

"Oh, you make me sick!" he blurted and stumbled away.

She laughed. "Great snappy comeback, Hank!"

However, Maggie wasn't in the clear yet. Mitch thought it might be a good idea for Camden to take her home.

"WT goes into the mad-mode with droolers and mewlers," he explained.

"I noticed," she answered. "What's his problem anyway?"

Mitch shrugged. "Dunno. He's mono-minded about all four-footers."

"Okay," she finally agreed. "I'll take her home. C'mon, Maggie."

But her cat was already halfway down the hall. Camden stopped at the door leading to the gloomy basement. She turned back to her friends.

"I haven't given up on finding out about that power-unit thing, you know!"

But no one answered her.

Maggie wouldn't say much on the way home. She wouldn't even stick her head out of the backpack. Camden didn't blame her.

"Magg, I'm sorry I took you there and I'm sorry that guy was mean to you and I promise I'll never take you back there again."

That was just fine with Maggie.

"I still can't get over being shrunk like that," Camden continued. "I wonder how he does those things. And what *is* that power-unit?"

There was no reply from within the backpack, so Camden had to think about it all by herself.

8

Grownies

AT DINNER that night, Camden almost told her parents about The Game. She had been frightened in that flat, desolate desert, and thinking about her parents had helped so much. She wished she could thank them.

"So how was the movie today?" her mother asked as she dipped a large spoonful of something that vaguely resembled casserole onto her daughter's plate.

"Movie?" Camden looked at her blankly. "Oh! The movie!"

That's what she'd written on the note — that she and Mitch were going to a movie. Darn! thought Camden. Now I'm going to have to make something up.

"Uh . . ." She stumbled for a moment. "It was, uh, some little kids' cartoon movie. It was so stupid we left."

Her mother gave her an odd look and Camden knew she wasn't buying it. She and Mitch loved movies, any kind, even little kids'.

"What was the title?" her mother asked sharply.

Camden took a gulp of milk, buying time.

"Oh, I can't remember. It was something about a lady mouse who fights a dragon. You know. They're all alike."

Mrs. Douglas frowned, studying her daughter.

She knows, Camden thought. She knows I'm faking it.

"Did this new friend of yours from Venice go too?" her mother asked.

Camden groaned silently. Oh great, she thought, now Dad will have a major grownie freak-out about Venice.

"Venice?" he asked, right on cue. "You have a friend who lives in Venice?"

"Yes," she answered defensively. "It's not illegal, you know."

He glanced up, surprised at her response.

"I don't think I like that tone of voice," he said sharply.

"Sorry," she answered. "But I can't help it if my friend lives in Venice. You act like it's a double ungood mondo-crime or something."

He raised an eyebrow.

"You'd better not get an attitude with me, young lady," he warned.

"All right, all right," Camden mumbled. "Don't have an attack."

Her father glared at her.

"I don't know what's gotten into you," he said angrily. "But this behavior is inexcusable at the dinner table!"

Camden leaped up.

"Fine! I wasn't hungry anyway!"

She glanced over at her mother, who was nervously mashing her beans into mush. Camden grabbed her plate, stomped into the kitchen, and threw out most of her dinner. Then she ran upstairs to the relative safety of her own room.

Camden closed the door solidly. They wouldn't allow her to lock it, but at least it was a barrier against them.

"Grownies!" she muttered.

Camden sat on her bed, leaning against the headboard. She grabbed her pillow and hugged it tight. This was all her mother's fault. She didn't *have* to mention Venice.

"Thanks a lot, Mother!" Camden said to the door angrily.

"Maw?" came the questioning answer from the other side.

"Maggie!"

Camden hopped off the bed to let her cat in.

"Am I glad to see you," she greeted Maggie, "because I'm double mad!"

Maggie jumped lightly onto Camden's dresser and became very involved in the serious business of grooming herself. But she politely cocked one ear to listen. Camden went back to her pillow.

"Parents are just so unfair sometimes," she told her cat. "It's okay for them to get all mad or huffy or moody or whatever they feel like. But if kids do, it suddenly becomes an 'attitude.'"

Maggie agreed that it wasn't fair. But she thought Camden's parents were reasonable about most things.

"Sure, they're reasonable," Camden answered. "As long as they get their own way. But once they feel the control slipping away, they just pull rank to get it back. It basically comes down to 'I'm the parent and you're the kid. I'm the boss and you're the slave!'"

Maggie thought Camden was exaggerating a little.

"I'm not exaggerating!" she protested. Camden was getting more and more upset about the unfairness of it all.

"We really don't have any rights, you know. It's kids against adults and the adults always win just because they're adults. WT-3 is right. It's us against them! Kidsters versus grownies!"

Maggie bristled at the mention of WT-3. She had a very bad feeling about him.

"Now I'm glad I didn't tell them about The Game," Camden mumbled. "They don't deserve to know about it."

Maggie didn't think Camden should make quick judgments about her parents just because of WT-3. After all, they were pretty nice, for people.

Camden sighed. "I know, but it's not easy being a kid, you know. We have no rights."

Maggie would have laughed if she could. What exactly did Camden think it was like being a cat? Never talk to a cat about rights!

Camden giggled and picked her up, scratching her in just the right place under her chin.

"You always know how to cheer me up," she said, hugging her tight. Maggie's purr kicked in loud and strong.

9

A Secret Meeting

LATE THAT NIGHT, snuggled in bed, Camden was delighted to find herself riding the Star Wind again. Over and under and up and around, past stars and galaxies and strange twinkling, tumbling waterfalls of light. Camden hoped she would never stop dreaming this dream.

Then, as before, she found herself approaching that peculiar glowing bronze sun, coming closer and closer until she could see the small planet. She glided slowly down toward the city of the bronze-haired people.

The feeling of being an observer was exactly the same as it had been the first time she dreamed of this strange planet. There was no sound at all as she flowed down a neighborhood street. Camden marveled at how similar this alien street was to streets at home.

Well, it's your dream, you're making it all up, she told herself. What did you expect it to be like? *Star Trek?* Geez, you can really be dumb sometimes.

When Camden looked into the windows of the houses,

she felt like a peeping Tom. Then she thought, How can you be a peeping Tom in your own dream, stupid?

In one of the houses Camden could see a family sitting at a table with their heads resting in their hands. She couldn't tell what was going on. One of the kids shot his head up suddenly, looking very pleased with himself. He said something to the rest of them and they all got very excited. They jumped around, hugging each other, and clapped the kid on the back as if they were congratulating him. The father quickly wrote something down and then they all went back to serious thought, bronze-haired heads in hands.

Hmmm, Camden thought, must be some kind of game.

In another house Camden could see a man dressed in a tuxedo scribbling madly on a large blackboard while a woman in a long evening dress stood at the door waiting impatiently. Camden could make out the words "I will not park in the red zone" as the man wrote the sentence over and over down the length of the blackboard.

At the end of the street, Camden glided up to a darkened house that appeared to be empty. She wondered why the dream brought her here when no one was home. But she glided through the front door anyway and down a long, dark hallway.

"There's nobody here," Camden tried to say aloud before she remembered that this was a dream and she couldn't make a sound.

But then she looked up and saw light seeping through

the cracks of a trap door above her in the hallway ceiling. And the dream carried her up through the trap door into a secret attic room that was filled with smoke, dusty air, and lots of people. The sound came on full blast as she entered.

"This just can't go on!" a man announced. Camden remembered him from the first dream. He was the little man who had been punished with all those story problems in the Grand Classroom. He was seated at the head of a large table, his crumpled hat lying next to a tall glass of water.

"We can't let her get away with it," an unhappy woman answered.

"It's just going to get worse and worse," another man said. "There are rumors on the street that she's planning to raise taxes even further, to thirty words a month! That's a word a day from every man, woman, and child!"

The people in the room responded with shocked looks at one another.

"We have to put a stop to this madness!" the first woman yelled. "We'll kill her! Death to the Teacher! Death to the Teacher!" The woman pounded her fist on the table.

"No, no, no!" The little gentleman tried to regain order. "Stop it! Violence isn't the answer!"

"It's the only way!" someone yelled.

A young woman stood up suddenly.

"We're all going crazy from this." She spoke in a calm voice that quieted the room. "We must keep our heads. Violence only breeds more violence."

A huge, bearlike man in the back of the room stood up. "What do you know?" he asked in a deep, rough voice. "You're just like her! You're probably on her side! You're a teacher!"

"Yeah! Shut up, teacher!" somebody else yelled at her. The young woman's eyes widened as she looked at the suddenly hostile faces around her.

"Wait! Wait! Please!" The little gentleman had to shout to be heard. "We can't turn against each other! And we can't assume all teachers are like that horrible woman in the Hall of Learning." He banged on the table. "I'm a professor!" he declared proudly. "And I organized this meeting!"

The people grew quiet again. He had embarrassed them. The large man leaned over and gently touched the young woman's arm.

"I — I'm sorry," he said in his gruff voice. "I'm just so angry and . . . tired."

The pretty young teacher nodded bravely, holding back tears.

"So," the professor went on, "I think we all agree that killing the Teacher is not the answer to our problems. We'll have to find another way to get her out of power."

The unhappy woman spoke up again. "How can we get her out? *We* elected her in the first place. We didn't know she was going to go mad with power! And now she's protected by her special police. We're lost! There's no way out!"

The woman threw her head into her arms and sobbed. Camden heard someone whisper that the woman couldn't be blamed for being so upset. Her husband was doing twenty years of solitary research in the county library for refusing to pay the Word Tax.

"Surely we can think of something," the gruff-voiced man said. "Surely we have enough brainpower in this room alone to outsmart one crazy teacher."

"Well, we'd better do it soon," the young woman answered, "because we're running out of time. You know she doesn't accept the same word twice. Once a word is turned in for payment, it's used up. And there are only so many words in the world. After we've turned them all in, after she's bled us dry, *then* what will she want?"

The professor cleared his throat.

"That's why we must decide on a course of action immediately. I've called you all here because I want to start an underground resistance, a place for people to go who are running from the Word Police."

"And you can lead it!" someone shouted.

He started to answer but another man interrupted him.

"You can't lead a secret organization. The Teacher knows your face! She sentenced you in the Grand Classroom!"

The professor smiled, a twinkle sparkling in his eye.

"But what will she remember? A nervous, confused fool. She would never connect him to the witty English professor you see standing before you tonight!"

His audience chuckled. Even the sobbing woman managed a half-smile.

Suddenly Camden felt herself drifting out of the attic room. She was pulled out of the dark house and up away from the bronze planet. She zoomed into the velvet darkness of space and caught the Star Wind home.

When Camden woke up she didn't feel at all rested. It was still dark outside.

"Maggie."

She reached down with her foot to nudge her sleeping cat.

"Maggie, I had that dream again."

Her cat opened one eye very slightly.

"Oh dear, did I wake you?" Camden chuckled. "So sorry."

Maggie didn't think it was so funny. She hoped this wasn't going to become a habit.

"No, no," Camden answered. "Just listen to this dream. It was the same as before except the story went on from where it left off."

Maggie reluctantly agreed to hear the dream as long as she got a good tummy scratch as part of the bargain.

"Isn't that awful?" Camden asked, after she'd told her cat all about it. "What are those poor people going to do? That family I saw must have been trying to find a new word for the tax. It wasn't a game at all! And twenty years of research! Can you believe it?"

No, Maggie couldn't believe it and she really didn't care. It was only a dream, after all. Now could she go back to sleep?

"Fine, be that way," Camden told her and turned over, snuggling deep under the covers. But she lay awake for a long time, thinking of the plight of the bronze-planet people and that terrible Teacher.

10

French Toast and Roller Coasters

Camden woke to the sun streaming into her eyes and the smell of French toast tempting her nose. Her empty stomach grumbling, she threw on some clothes, brushed her teeth, and stumbled downstairs.

She couldn't figure out why her parents hadn't left for work until she remembered that it was Saturday. Camden heard them talking quietly in the breakfast nook and wondered if they were still mad from the night before.

"Morning, Bright Eyes!" her dad said cheerfully, rumpling her short, uncombed hair. "We were wondering when you were going to join the land of the living."

"I made French toast, honey," her mom said. "Think you could manage to swallow a few bites?"

French toast happened to be Camden's favorite food in the world and it was the only thing her mother made perfectly.

Guess they're not mad anymore, she thought.

The breakfast was her mother's way of smoothing things

over. Both her parents were trying to be nice, and Camden felt a little guilty for her outburst of the night before.

"Well," her dad said as she finished her third serving of French toast, "since your mother is leaving us this morning to go play Real Estate, it looks as if we're stuck with the dishes."

Camden had to admit that he had a knack for finding fun in the most boring chores. This morning he made a contest out of the dirty dishes. Her dad washed, Camden dried, and whoever finished last had to stand still for a swat with a wet dishrag. Camden won by a plate and a fork, but she thought he dropped that pan on purpose.

Looking humble and scared, he handed her the dishrag, closing his eyes to wait for the stinging swat. Camden wound it round and round, taking her time, then wound it some more.

When the dishrag was very tight and very wet she said, "Boy, this is a very tight dishrag and it's going to leave a nasty red mark that won't go away for days."

He clenched his eyes tighter and quoted from his favorite book. "It is a far, far better thing I do than I have ever done."

When she finally struck, it was a sloppy smack with hardly any snap on the end. However, his reaction was award-winning. He howled and screamed in agony and hopped around. Suddenly grabbing the dishrag out of her hands, he twisted it quickly and got off a good smack to her legs before she knew what hit her.

"No, no, unfair! Unfair!" she howled, leaping and side-stepping to avoid the snapping rag.

"Aha! Now let's see how you like it, my pretty!" he cackled in his best Wicked-Witch-of-the-West voice. "You're dancing to a different tune now, I see."

In response to all the ruckus, two little cat eyes peered around a corner. Maggie leaped to the kitchen counter, eager to be in on the fun.

"Maggie! Maggie! Help me! Help!" Camden called.

"Back off, you mangy, flea-infested feline," her father snarled. Maggie cocked an ear back. She was neither mangy nor flea-infested.

Camden's father snapped the dishrag at her. With a lightning stroke, Maggie shot out a gray paw and snagged the rag on a very sharp claw. It flew right out of her dad's hands, causing his jaw to drop in amazement. Then Maggie picked the rag up in her mouth and flashed out of the kitchen, a gray blur.

Camden and her dad stared at each other in amazement. Then they both fell into their chairs, laughing hysterically.

"You should have seen your face!" Camden sputtered.

"I always knew she was smart," he said, laughing, "but I had no idea that a mere cat could make me look so stupid."

Camden felt confused for a second. What did he say?

"What?" she asked, her laughter fading. "Make you look what?"

"Stupid!" he repeated, chuckling. "You know, completely dumb."

"Oh," she said, and the confused feeling was gone as quickly as it had come.

All of this drama was, of course, her father's way of making up. He always did something like that when he felt bad about an argument. And it was fun. But sometimes she wished he would just apologize straight out as other fathers did.

Mitch showed up after Mr. Douglas left for the golf course. He was ready to hit the road for Venice.

"Again?" Camden asked.

"Lezgo, CD-1," he said at the door. "WT doesn't like it when Kidsters are late."

"Mitch," she said, "there is no way I'm going back there again today. You wouldn't believe how mad my dad got last night."

He snorted. "Slugged-out grownies. Lezgo," he repeated.

Camden put her hands on her hips and stared at him.

"I can't, Mitch! Just forget it!" she said loudly. "Anyway, I'm not sure I want to play The Game again."

He sighed. "Why not?"

"I don't know." She shrugged. "I just — it's so strange. It gives me a funny feeling."

When he started to protest, she put up a hand to stop him.

"Besides," she continued, "I'm still mad at you about yesterday."

He groaned. "Okay, what'd I do?"

"Well," she answered, arms crossed. "First, you rode

away when I was trying to tell you about that book. And second, you acted like a sp—" She stopped.

"A what?" he demanded.

But she didn't want to hurt his feelings by calling him a spineless nerd.

"You act like you're afraid of WT-3," she answered tactfully.

"I do not!" he yelled.

They stared at each other angrily for a couple of minutes. Finally he mumbled, "I just want to learn The Words, that's all. Now are you coming or not?"

"I really can't, Mitch," she answered, and they seemed to be friends again. "But at least stay long enough to hear about this bizarre dream I've been having."

"Make it double quick," he answered, leaning against the door.

"Well," she began, talking fast, "it's the best dream and it always starts off where it finished the night before. See, there's always this wild wind that takes me on a fantastic ride, like a roller coaster only better, and —"

"What?" He stopped her.

She looked at him. "What what?"

"That last part," he said.

She was getting confused. "The roller coaster part?"

"Roller coas . . . ter?" he repeated as if he had absolutely no idea what she was talking about.

"Yeah, Mitch, roller coaster. You know, like at amusement parks, lots of high-speed turns, kids screaming, you think you're going to upchuck. *You* know," she prodded him.

But Camden didn't see the light dawn on his face.

"C'mon, Mitch, are you kidding or what?" she asked.

"Oh, yeah, right," he answered finally. "A roller coaster."

But she could tell he was faking it. He really didn't know what a roller coaster was! She could see a very troubled look in his eye.

Mitch got up suddenly without a word. He grabbed his bike and started to ride away.

"Mitch!" she called after him.

"Double-bye," he answered softly and pedaled away without so much as a wave.

Camden thought about that for a long time. Mitch used to know what a roller coaster was. She couldn't remember how many times they'd been on them together. What was the matter with him? Was he losing his mind? She shook her head and wondered how a person could just forget what a roller coaster was. It wasn't as if it was a dull, boring thing. She would have understood if he forgot what a rake was or a garbage disposal or something. But a roller coaster? She shook her head again.

On Monday morning Mitch called Camden bright and early. She hadn't seen him since that Saturday.

"CD-1," he said when she answered the phone.

It took her a second to understand what he meant.

"CD-1? Are you there?" he asked.

"Oh! The Words! Yes, MM-3, I'm here," she answered.

"So have you been hanging with your grownies or what?" he asked.

"Uh, yep," she said. "It was okay though. We went to the beach, and we saw this really cosmic movie about a little alien from space who —"

But he cut her off.

"The Kidsters noticed a void where your unit should be, especially WT-3. He wants to know if you're going to pull a repeat no-show today."

"A no-show?" she asked.

"Do you want to hang with us or not, Camden?" he asked, with a slight edge to his voice.

"Well," she answered, "I have to ask my parents — I mean grownies. Call you back."

"Double-bye." He hung up.

No mention of the roller coaster thing that happened Saturday. She decided to try to get permission to go. After all, Mitch said they'd all missed her. And, anyway, she was falling behind on The Words. That stupid Hank would make fun of her if she didn't know what they were saying.

Camden fiddled with the spiral phone cord. No, there was more to it than that. She really wanted to play The Game again. In fact, she'd been thinking about it all weekend. It was kind of an urge she felt, a little like those times when she absolutely couldn't go another minute without a chocolate bar. Yes, that was it. She had a real craving to play The Game.

Camden found her dad in the kitchen, all suited up with a tie, eating an English muffin over the sink.

"Mmmmmmmph," he said to Camden.

"Morning, Dad. Going to court today?" she asked, putting a muffin into the toaster.

"Mmmmmm, big trial." He nodded, chewing quickly.

Bravely she plunged in.

"Would it be okay for me to go to Venice with Mitch after I do my chores?"

He swallowed. "Where in Venice and to do what?" he asked, always the attorney.

"Well, remember the guy I mentioned the other night who lives there?" she asked.

"Mmmmmmm," he said with a nod, taking another bite.

"Well, I don't know his exact address there, but I can find out," she answered.

"To do what?" he repeated.

Camden considered this for a minute. Finally she answered, hoping that he'd take it as a joke, "To hang out with my peer group."

It worked. He laughed.

"Okay, okay, that's good. You got me. No objection, counselor. But find out his address and phone number when you get there and leave it with the service in case we need you. And stay with Mitch! Fair enough?" he asked, wiping his hands quickly.

"Fair enough," she answered. "Thanks, Dad. And try to have a good day slaving over a hot witness stand!"

She heard him chuckle as he grabbed his briefcase and ran out the door.

Maggie was no problem. She wouldn't go back to that nasty hotel with those horrible people for anything, not even for two whole bags of Fritos!

11

The Door-Unit

WHEN CAMDEN AND MITCH arrived at the (Something) View Arms, she remembered that she had promised to get the address and phone number for her dad. But Mitch told her that she'd have to do a pass on the phone because WT-3 didn't even own one. They were grownie-units. And he wouldn't go find a pay phone with her, either.

"Just forget about it, CD-1," he told her.

"But I'll get in trouble, Mitch," she complained.

He sneered. "Grownie trouble!"

"Who cares what kind it is?" she answered. "It's still trouble."

But he still wouldn't go with her.

"I refuse to help you follow grownie orders," he stated flatly and walked down the steps without her.

"Fine. Be that way," she said after he'd gone. "But don't tell me you're not afraid of WT-3."

It took a while for Camden's eyes to adjust to the dim light of the hotel lobby when she returned from following "grownie orders." She could see the profile of a tall figure surrounded by the Kidsters as she hurried to join the circle.

WT glanced up at her arrival.

"CD-1." He smiled in that unfriendly way of his. "Heard you were snagged in Grownieville. That's a too badness."

"Yeah, well" — she shrugged — "I'm here now."

"Lezgo," he commanded, holding up the dull gray power cube. "Do The Game!"

Camden felt a thrill of excitement as the circle of Kidsters began to move around WT, and she didn't hold back at all as she felt herself being drawn into that black, spinning vacuum.

This time, when her vision cleared, Camden found herself looking down at her own shadow. She knew it was hers because of its shape. She'd seen it following along behind her many times before like a faithful friend. She raised her arm and lowered it just to make sure. The shadow mirrored her movement exactly. Camden looked again. There seemed to be something different about it. Her shadow seemed bigger than before. In fact, it stretched out along the ground at least two or three times as tall as Camden. She moved her other arm. When she lowered it the shadow followed her movement obediently.

But isn't a shadow supposed to move at *exactly* the same time as the person? she wondered.

Camden's shadow seemed to be watching, waiting for her to make a move before it followed. She bent to the right and back up. The shadow waited. Camden counted one-two-three before it bent to the right and back up again. She kicked out a leg, shook her foot, and drew it back.

One-two-three-four. Her shadow finally lifted one leg, shook its foot, and drew it back.

Odd, Camden thought. Very odd.

Then the shadow threw up its arms and twirled around. Camden hadn't moved an inch. One-two-three, she counted. Suddenly she felt an overwhelming urge to throw up her arms, and she was twirling around exactly as her shadow had done.

It marched to the right, left, right, and Camden did the same, right, left, right, like a puppet on a string. The shadow leaped into the air, kicked its heels, and flipped over into a cartwheel. Before she knew it, Camden was in the air, kicking her heels and executing a perfect cartwheel. She giggled. Camden had never before done a successful cartwheel in her life. She always fell over at the last minute.

Then they were away. Whirling and hopping, leaping and twisting, Camden followed her shadow in a wild crazy dance. She looked up to see Mitch twirling past on his toes. Camden chuckled to herself because Mitch hated to dance.

After a long time, Camden's lungs began to ache and she tried to slow down just a little. But the shadow held her tightly in its grip and wouldn't let her go. Finally, mercifully, Camden welcomed that heavy drowsiness that she knew would bring an end to the frenzy. As her eyelids drooped, Camden felt her shadow release her, and she watched it twirl away, twisting and leaping, as if it had found its own freedom at last.

*   *   *

Camden sat up and wiped the grit from her hands.

"Not the *most* fun I've ever had," she commented, rubbing her tired legs. She looked around and noticed that the others were just beginning to wake up.

Now's my chance, she thought.

Getting quietly to her feet, Camden tiptoed very carefully over to the staircase. She was determined to find that door-unit thing that nobody would tell her about. She climbed slowly toward the second floor, checking behind her quickly when she stepped on a squeaky stair. But no one noticed as she slipped around the corner and entered a faded hallway with a long row of doors. Peeking through one of them, Camden found a single square, empty room with nothing inside but dust and old newspapers. Her head throbbed painfully, but she tried to ignore it.

Following WT's footprints in the dust, she continued down the hall past more doors and more rooms, up another staircase and down another long hallway. On the third floor, Camden was closely following the footprints around a corner when she ran smack into a very strange staircase that stuck right up out of the middle of the floor.

The wooden staircase looked very steep and wobbly. It seemed to have been thrown together at the very last minute. The stairs curved almost straight up, tilting to one side. She could see a door on a small landing at the top.

Now this is very odd, she said to herself. Very, very odd. Why would a hotel for senior citizens have a steep, rickety staircase that looks as though it would be tough for a serious athlete to climb? And what could possibly be behind that door at the top? Another little stuffy room? She doubted it. Suddenly Camden realized that she must have stumbled upon the door-unit that everybody was so secretive about. She grinned to herself. I am so smart, she thought.

Just then the door at the top of the strange staircase creaked open. Camden scurried into one of the rooms and peeked through the crack at the edge of the door. But her view was blocked and she could see only part of the way up the stairs. Camden heard the sound of locks locking and bolts bolting heavily into place. Boy, she thought, whatever lies behind that door must be very valuable.

Then Camden heard the familiar sound of boots pounding down the steps. Soon she was able to see WT-3's jeaned legs as they came into her view. No big surprise. He stopped at the bottom of the staircase, fixed his cap, and stomped out of her sight.

Now the question lay before her. Was she going up those stairs to check out that door or was she going to play it safe? Camden decided that safe is not the stuff of which adventures are made. Besides, her curiosity was killing her. She tiptoed quietly to the shaky stairs and started up, head still pounding.

As Camden placed her weight on the bottom step, she felt the entire structure sway and wobble as if it were tacked together with bubble gum. Whoever built this ought to go back to builder's school, she thought. But Camden hugged the splintery banister and kept climbing.

She finally reached the landing at the top and stared at the door. The only way she could tell it was really a door was by the rusty hinges and the tarnished brass doorknob. The rest of it was a jumble, a mix-and-match jigsaw puzzle of pieces of wood that looked as though they'd been borrowed from here and there. The pieces were all of different colors, some freshly painted, some peeling. The way it was tacked together this way and that reminded Camden of her grandmother's ancient patchwork quilt. It was strange and different from any other door in the whole building.

Camden could see that the four old locks had been attached quickly by someone who had no idea how to attach locks. The screws hadn't been screwed in all the way and the leftover parts had been hammered sideways. Camden didn't think it would be too tough to break in. But she wouldn't have felt right about that.

Stuck, she thought. Stuck, stuck, stuck. I'm dying to know what WT's got behind there. But short of breaking the door down, there was no way for her to find out. Camden had no choice but to turn around and go back. Besides, her head was killing her.

She made her way carefully down the wobbly steps. Maybe that door doesn't lead anywhere so special, she thought. Maybe it's just a plain ol' door after all. But it sure doesn't look like any ol' door. And that didn't explain the stairway or the reason that WT wouldn't let anyone inside. Mmmmm, she thought, curiouser and curiouser.

The gang was up and babbling when she reached the top of the lobby staircase. She quickly slipped down to mix with the group. WT hadn't noticed her absence. But when he saw her he darted a nervous glance up the stairs. Camden quickly turned to chat with Nancy, trying to act casual.

"Hey, my stomach's doing a meltdown on me here," Danny complained.

"What'd he say?" Camden asked Mitch.

"He's hungry," he told her.

Everybody packed up and headed out together. But Camden noticed that WT-3 stayed behind.

"Isn't WT coming?" she asked.

"No, he always does a pass when we go out," Nancy answered.

"Why?"

"Dunno. He says munch markets and sand lizards make him mondo-crazed and he can't deal with all the lame grownies."

"Oh," she said, figuring that munch markets were fast-food joints and sand lizards must be those people who lie around in the sun all day getting wrinkled.

WT stood all alone in the shadows of the empty lobby watching them leave, his profile framed against the dusty light. Camden wondered what brought him here and whether he was really as tough as he seemed. She wondered where his family was and whether he ever got homesick late at night. Just for a moment, Camden almost felt sorry for him.

12

A Shiverdrooler with No Tears and a Poke

NANCY, Dan, Mitch, and Camden pedaled over to the Santa Monica pier. But it was summer in Venice and all their favorite munch markets were stacked twenty feet deep with tourists. Then someone noticed a sign in a local restaurant window that said: SPECIAL!!! ALL YOU CAN EAT $2.50!!

"Kidsters, look! We can do a mondo-munchout at that place for cheap."

"Do we have enough paper?" Danny asked.

"Paper?" Camden didn't understand what he meant.

"Paper, green paper," Mitch explained. "You know, money."

"Oh."

They pooled their green paper and found that they just barely had enough. That decided, they stormed into the restaurant but had to wait in the lobby for the hostess to seat them. They waited, then waited some more. Feeling ignored, Danny tried to get the hostess's attention, but she breezed right past them, too busy to notice his wildly waving arm. However, two minutes after a man and his wife came in the door, the hostess appeared, all smiles.

"Table for two?" she asked the couple. The woman looked at the kids.

"Uh, I think these young people were here before us," she said politely.

The hostess pinched her lips together.

"Oh," she said. "Okay, c'mon, you kids."

She led them to a booth in the back of the restaurant, threw a couple of menus down, and pranced off to seat the man and woman.

"Typical grownie attitude," Nancy remarked.

None of them bothered to pick up the menu.

"Does everybody know what they want?" Camden asked.

They did. But no waitress appeared to take their order.

"Can you believe this?" Mitch said. "Ignored or what?"

Finally a scowling waitress walked over, chewing her gum loudly.

"No separate checks!" she announced.

"Fine, no big," Mitch answered. "We're going to do the All-You-Can-Munch Special anyway."

Camden and Nancy giggled. The waitress stared at them until they stopped laughing. Then she turned to look at the clock on the wall behind her.

"Special's over at five o'clock," she said lazily. "It's five."

Camden leaned around her to look at the clock. It read 4:57.

"It's four fifty-seven," she protested. "We still have three minutes."

The waitress smiled a sickly sweet smile and looked at the clock again.

"Fine," she said. "So you have three minutes. Make it snappy."

"Right," Camden answered, and everyone started ordering at once.

"One at a time!" the waitress yelled. She pointed her pencil at Nancy.

"You," she demanded. "What'll it be?"

Nancy ordered as fast as she could.

"A shiverdrooler with no tears and a poke."

The waitress poised her pencil to write, then stopped and glared at her.

"What?"

Everyone giggled.

Finally Mitch came to the rescue.

"Uh, she wants a . . . uh, a chili dog without onions and a . . . a Coke."

The waitress raised an eyebrow.

"Right," she said writing it down. She pointed her pencil at Danny.

He said, "A double humbleburgle with crispies and a poke."

She sighed and looked at the clock.

"What do you want, in English?" she asked.

They giggled again. Mitch translated again.

"He wants a . . . a double hamburgle, I mean burger, with, uh, crispies . . . uh . . ." He couldn't seem to remember the right grownie word.

"French fries?" Camden asked. She'd never heard this part of The Words before. It was fun.

"Yeah, right, fries," Mitch said. "And a Coke."

"Sure," the waitress answered, snapping her gum. She pointed her pencil at Mitch.

"You got one minute."

The words flew out. "A plain drooler with Hitchcock and nilla quake."

Hand on a hip, the waitress cocked her head to one side and didn't even bother writing. The others were trying very hard to keep their faces straight.

"Oh," Mitch said. "Uh, I mean, I want a plain hot dog and . . . and, uh, a . . ." he stumbled.

Camden was trying hard to figure out all these new Kidster words. Nilla quake? Quake — rhymes with . . .

"Shake! Vanilla shake!" she announced triumphantly.

The waitress had decided that these kids were completely out of their minds. But she scribbled it down anyway. Nancy and Dan had buried their faces, laughing into their arms.

The waitress looked at the clock.

"Thirty seconds and counting," she said, pointing the pencil at Camden.

"Uh, I want —" Camden wanted to try to order in The Words, but she had to do it fast. "I would like a humble-burgle with crispies and a poke."

"You mean like this?"

The waitress poked Camden in the arm with the eraser end of the pencil and laughed harshly.

Camden yelped. "Ow!"

"Hey, you can't do that!" Mitch yelled. Camden rubbed the sore spot.

The waitress shrugged.

"Just kidding. So what does *she* want? You got about two seconds."

Mitch answered angrily, spitting the words at her: "She wants a hamburger, French fries, and a Coke!"

The waitress casually looked over her shoulder at the clock and exclaimed with fake sorrow, "Oh, look at that! It's one minute after five. Special's over; too bad. Regular prices from five till nine."

A group moan escaped from the table. They didn't have enough money to pay for it all without the Special.

Camden blew up.

"What are you talking about, lady?" she demanded, rubbing her arm. "We walked in here at least twenty minutes before five. We waited ten minutes for someone even to notice us at the door, then we had to wait another ten before you could bother to drag yourself over. We gave you our order as fast as we could and now you say it's too late for the Special. That is just not fair!"

Camden had a thing for fairness.

"Yeah!" the Kidsters agreed loudly.

The usual clanking of silverware and conversation in the restaurant had dropped off and the people were beginning to notice the ruckus.

"It's your double ungood grownie ways and slugged-out thinking against Kidsters, that's all it is!" Dan announced.

"What?" the waitress asked, darting a nervous glance around the room. She whispered at them in a harsh voice, "You kids just better keep it down or I'll have you thrown out of here!"

"But we haven't done anything," Camden protested.

"You come in here and play your games and take me away from regular paying customers," she told them.

"We have money, we're paying customers!" Camden said in their defense. The restaurant had become very quiet.

"Right, this has been a total double badness from the start and our paper is just as good as grownies'!" Nancy told her.

"And we didn't even order on separate checks!" Camden added.

"Is there a problem, Beulah?" a calm male voice asked from behind her.

The waitress whipped around to face a short man in a suit.

Must be the manager, Camden thought.

"No, no problem, Mr. Sterne. I've got it under control," she answered hastily. "Just a bunch of kids come in here to give us trouble."

"We're not giving her trouble!" Camden tried to explain. "We just wanted to get our food with the Special. But we had to wait twenty minutes before we could get anyone's attention. By the time she showed up it was almost too late. Now she says we have to pay regular prices!"

Camden's parents had taught her to stand up for her rights.

"Well, you didn't even speak in English," the waitress yelled at her.

"Well, you poked me with your pencil and my arm still hurts!" Camden yelled back.

Mr. Sterne turned to the waitress.

"Is that true, Beulah?" he demanded.

Camden held up her arm to show him the nasty red mark.

Beulah's face was beginning to turn a blotchy pink color.

"Well, these stupid kids were giving me a hard time and they weren't really trying to order, they were just causing trouble."

"We ordered!" everybody yelled.

Mr. Sterne took over, trying to save the situation from complete disaster.

"All right, all right, everyone stay calm." He smiled at the other customers. "No problem, everyone go back to your meal. Everything's fine here," he announced to the entire restaurant. Then his customer's smile turned to ice as he glared at Beulah.

"Look on her pad," Mitch told him. "Our order's right there."

Mr. Sterne grabbed it out of her hand.

"A double hamburger, French fries . . ." He practically threw it back at her. "It looks like English to me. Now just make their orders, give them the Special prices, and I want to speak to you after you've finished your shift."

The Kidsters applauded as Beulah walked away with a

brightly flushed face. The manager apologized to the kids and beamed smiles at the curious diners.

"Oooooh, she is in double trouble," said Nancy, laughing.

"Serves her right, treating us like droolers," Danny said.

Mitch chuckled. "The Words really got her, though. She's so vacuum-packed she didn't even know what hit her."

"Well, you guys almost got me, too," Camden admitted. "I think I figured out most of it. But what's Hitchcock?"

"Hitchcock? You know, that red stuff in all those scary Hitchcock movies that's supposed to look like blood," Mitch answered.

"Oh! Ketchup!" Camden said. "And I figured out quake because it rhymes with shake — too easy. And crispies are fries and a double humbleburgle is so obvious."

The waitress appeared with their food in probably record time for the restaurant and she actually got the orders right. But she refused to speak to them and avoided the Kidster table like the plague. They decided to be generous, tipping her handsomely with a quarter, and didn't even leave it under an upside-down glass of water.

13

WT-3 Does a Pass on Two Grownies

*F*OR THE NEXT FEW WEEKS, Camden went back to Venice whenever she could get away with it. Most times, she just didn't mention where she'd been that day. But sometimes she had to lie outright to her parents. Camden knew it was wrong, but she just had to play The Game. Her parents wouldn't understand and she didn't feel like arguing about it.

Mitch went every day, even on weekends. For that reason, Camden didn't learn The Words as fast as he did and she always felt she was behind the others. Sometimes they even made fun of her when she used too many grownie words. They pretended they didn't know what she was talking about. That didn't seem fair. After all, she was learning as fast as she could.

Also, Camden thought WT would teach them The Words. But that wasn't how it worked at all. The Kidsters were expected to pick up the new language just by hanging around him and using it among themselves. Camden thought it would have been easier to write The Words down. But WT considered that method too grownie.

The Game was different every time. Camden still couldn't figure out how WT did it or what the power-unit was. But after a while she really didn't care anymore. She found herself thinking about The Game all the time, wondering what the next strange new experience was going to be. Sometimes The Game was pure fun, light and easy, and sometimes it was wild and frightening. But she always wanted to play it, no matter what. And on the days when she got stuck at home that uncomfortable craving would gnaw at her. She really missed The Game on those days. More than that, she needed it.

The only really bad thing was the headache. It grew steadily worse and worse every time she played The Game. The other Kidsters got it, too. Camden was always relieved when her head stopped throbbing. There was a pleasant kind of blankness when it was over, like an empty spot where the headache had been. But The Game was worth it.

One afternoon, a very strange thing happened at the (Something) View Arms. The Kidsters were just waking up from The Game and WT had vanished somewhere up the stairs, as usual.

"MM-3," Camden asked Mitch, "what's WT going to do when the school month comes and we have to do time in prison-class?"

"Double don't know," he shrugged. "He'll go into the mad-mode, I guess."

Camden laughed. "That's a trueness!"

"Shhhhhhh!" Marvin shushed everyone. "Shhhhhhhhh!" he whispered. "Someone's trying to get in!"

Everyone shut up instantly. Sure enough, the Kidsters heard voices outside. Frozen, they stared at the door as the boards were pulled off and a key worked at the locks.

"Hide!" somebody whispered.

The Kidsters were out of sight in seconds. The front door creaked open and two men stepped into the dim, littered lobby.

"Grownies," Camden heard Hank mutter from somewhere behind her. She had found a hiding place in a small closet under the staircase.

The men were talking loudly, shining their flashlights into the dusty shadows.

"How long has the building been empty?" one of them asked.

"Oh, I think we got the last of the old folks out about six months ago," the other one answered. As they came closer, Camden could see that they were both wearing gray suits and shiny shoes.

"I figure it'll take about six weeks to gut the place and tear it down."

"Hey, look at this!" One of them had found Kidster footprints. "Somebody's been making himself at home here!"

"You're right," the other man answered. "Footprints all over the place!"

Camden held her breath. Her nose was starting to tickle from the dust in the tiny closet. She was dying to sneeze, but somebody else beat her to it.

"AAAAAH! AAAAH! CHOOO!"

The two men looked at each other.

"All right, come on out! We know you're here!" one of them said.

No one moved.

They found Sara first and dragged her out from behind a crate.

"All right, kid. Come on, let's go!"

Sara tried to wriggle away, but one of the men grabbed her by the shoulders, shaking her back and forth.

"What do you think you're doing in here, you little brat?" he shouted in her face. "Don't you know this is private property?"

"Are there any other kids here with you?" the other man demanded.

Sara shook her head.

"Little liar!" the first one yelled. "I know you're not poking around here all by yourself! Now tell me where your friends are hiding!" He started jerking her back and forth again.

"Take your rotten grownie hands off her!" Mitch demanded, stepping out from behind a door. Camden followed right behind him. Then one by one the rest of the Kidsters came out of hiding. Soon the two men were staring at a group of fifteen angry Kidsters.

"Good Lord!" one of them declared. "It's a gang!"

Camden could see that the idea of a gang had them worried. They released Sara and backed up a few steps.

"Double ungood grownies!" Hank growled at them. "We won't let you take us back to the prison-school! We won't!"

The men gasped. "Prison?"

"These kids must be juvenile delinquents!" one of them whispered.

"Wonder how long they've been holed up here?" the other one asked nervously.

"I don't know. But I think we'd better get out of here and call the police."

"You're right." One of them cleared his throat. "All right, you kids!" he yelled with a slight quiver in his voice. "This is private property! You'd better clear out right now because we're calling the police!"

Then they both turned around and headed toward the door. Camden could tell that they were trying not to hurry.

Without warning, WT appeared out of the shadows. He stepped right out in front of them, blocking their way. In his hand the power-unit spun and twirled as he held it up in front of their eyes.

The two men stopped dead in their tracks and stared into that spinning blackness. No one made a sound as the Kidsters watched, holding their breath. After several long minutes WT slipped silently away with the power-unit still spinning in his hand.

The two men jerked suddenly. Then, to Camden's astonishment, they went right on talking as if absolutely nothing had happened. And they didn't say anything about the police or the Kidsters or WT or any of them.

"Okay, well, everything's fine here," one of them said.

"Yep. Doesn't look like anyone's been in the building since the tenants left," the other one answered.

"What do you say to a beer?"

"Sounds good to me."

The men flashed their lights over the darkened lobby one more time, catching the astonished faces of the Kidsters in the beams. Then they walked out, locking the door behind them.

After a long silence, the Kidsters broke into a cheer. Laughing, hooting, and hollering, they clapped WT-3 on the back.

"Mondo-cosmic, WT!"

"You did a major pass on those ungood grownies!"

Camden watched WT uneasily for a few minutes before she gathered her courage and marched straight up to him.

"What did you do to them?" she demanded. "One minute they were going to call the police, and the next minute they acted like they had never even seen us!"

WT glanced at her. "Forget it, CD-1," he said quietly.

But Camden wouldn't forget it. The whole thing was so strange and unnatural it made her nervous. It was one thing for weird stuff to happen in a kid's game. But when that stuff happened to real adults, it brought a cold splash of reality into the Kidsters' secret world. She shook her head.

"I want to know what you did to them!" she demanded.

Standing nearby, Hank decided it was time to butt in.

"Unlax, CD-1!" he told her. "You always get mondo-crazed."

"Yeah," Mark agreed. "WT did it, that's all. Do a pass on the whys and hows."

Camden bit her lip as WT smiled that cool smile. He leaned down to whisper in her ear.

"I took them."

Surprised, Camden looked up at him. "Took what?"

"The thoughts," he answered simply and walked away.

She stared after him. Took the thoughts? What thoughts? She scratched her head, trying to figure out what he meant by that. The two grownies had started talking about beer and stuff as if they had completely forgotten about the Kidsters. The Kidsters? Did he take the thoughts of the Kidsters out of their heads so they wouldn't remember seeing anybody in the building? Camden shook her head. No, that was impossible.

But the two men never returned in all the time Camden spent at the (Something) View Arms.

After that, Camden would sneak back up the rickety stairs whenever she could. She was certain that WT was more than he appeared to be and that the secret lay behind that door. But WT always locked it when he came out, and she could never get a good look inside. She asked Mitch if he knew anything about the door-unit.

He frowned. "No, CD-1, and I don't want to know anything, either. WT-3 goes into the mad-mode when any Kidster goes up there."

"Thought he might," she answered.

"What's the big?" he asked. "A room's a room, a door's a door, a bore's a bore." Pleased with his rhyme, he wandered away.

What is the matter with him? Camden wondered. It's like he doesn't have any curiosity anymore or interest in anything except WT and The Game. Neither of them ever talked about books the way they used to. Mitch never built models anymore. He used to be better than anyone else at video games. Now he couldn't care less. He didn't even like to go swimming now. They never did anything but hang out at WT-3's. Mitch had changed, that was for sure — and sometimes Camden wondered if maybe she had, too.

14

More Trouble at Home

CAMDEN HAD a headache that night after dinner, and she just wanted to go to bed. But her parents insisted that she play a game of Scrabble with them.

"C'mon, honey, we haven't played Scrabble since the day you got home from camp," her mother said.

Camden rolled her eyes. There was no getting out of it.

"So, Cammie, read any good books lately?" her father asked as he spelled out LITERATURE on the Scrabble board.

"Well, no," she answered. "I'm still working on *The Jungle Books*." She couldn't think of a word to spell with her letters.

"You haven't finished *The Jungle Books* yet?" he asked with surprise.

Camden was a fast reader. She usually whipped through a book, especially one she liked.

"I thought you loved Kipling," her mother remarked, placing her letters to read NOVEL.

"I do," Camden answered. But she hadn't picked up the

book in over a month. Reading just didn't seem like much fun these days. It was too much work or something.

"I guess I haven't been in the read-mode lately," she said.

"Read-mode?" her mom repeated, chuckling. "That's cute, Camden."

It was Camden's turn to play and she still hadn't decided on a word to spell with her letters. Finally she placed the tiles to read BOOK.

"Is that the best you can do?" her father asked.

"It's all I could come up with," she answered defensively.

"It's a perfectly fine word," her mom added, patting her on the leg.

"Well," her dad continued, "I hope you get back to Mowgli the wolf boy before his feelings get hurt."

Camden smiled as she watched him spell out PARAGRAPH on the game board.

"No, I won't do a total pass," Camden answered.

Her dad silently mouthed the words "total pass" at his wife. She shrugged.

Mrs. Douglas spelled out CHARACTER with the tiles. Then it was Camden's turn again.

The game wasn't going well. She was losing badly. Camden shifted nervously and looked over at her parents. They were playing kissy-face while they waited for Camden to take her turn.

Yecccech, she said to herself and used her letters to spell out GROWNIE on the board.

Her father looked at the word.

"Grownie?" he asked. "What's that?"

"You know," she answered without thinking. "It's you guys, grownies, grownups."

"Grownies?" they asked.

"Grownies?" her father repeated. "Actually, I probably would have loved that word when I was a kid." He turned to Camden. "But I'm not a kid, so get it off the board!"

"All right, all right, don't get insulted," Camden answered. She took a look at the word, then removed the I and E.

"There," she said, sitting back. "Happy?"

"Besides," her mom added, "you know you can't use slang in this game, honey."

"Or in this house, for that matter," her father said. "Where did you get that word anyway? Because I really"— he spelled out the letters on the Scrabble board — "D, E, S, P, I, S, E it!"

"Just around," Camden answered, feeling the tension level rise.

"Around where?" her dad asked.

"From the other Kidst — kids." She had almost said "Kidsters" but stopped herself just in time. She didn't think it would go over very well right now.

"So does that mean you have to use it, too?" he demanded. Camden felt as though she were on trial.

"No," she answered.

"Then why do you use that word?" he asked, the game forgotten.

"Because I want to!" she snapped, very close to tears.

"And you want to just because the other kids do, right?" he cross-examined.

Camden's head was pounding and her father was only making it worse.

"No, Dad," she snapped. "I use slang just because I know you don't like it!"

Camden sucked in her breath, surprised at her own outburst. Then the tears broke and she fled up the stairs to her room, slamming the door behind her.

Through her sobbing, Camden could hear the loud machine-gun patter of angry words from below. But she didn't care enough to listen.

There was something wrong. Camden didn't know if the wrong was with her father or with herself. But there was a painful bruise inside of her that wouldn't go away.

The soft knock at Camden's door came a long time later. She sat up, grabbing her pillow.

"Camden? Are you all right?" It wasn't Maggie this time.

She cleared her throat and tried to sound normal. "Yes, Mom," she answered.

"May I come in?"

There was no way to avoid it.

"If you want," she mumbled in reply.

Mrs. Douglas entered quietly. She began fiddling with the things on Camden's dresser.

"Honey," she began, "is something the matter? Is there a problem you want to discuss?"

Here we go, Camden thought. She wants to have "a talk."

"No," she answered.

"Are you sure?" her mother prodded.

"Yes, I'm sure!" Camden flared at her. "What's the big deal?"

Mrs. Douglas turned to face her daughter sternly.

"There is no excuse for your behavior this evening," she said. "Your father and I would like an explanation."

"I'm sorry, okay?" Camden snapped.

Mrs. Douglas sat down on the edge of the bed. Camden noticed that her eyes looked tired.

"Please tell me what's wrong, honey," she pleaded.

Camden didn't answer right away. Then it all burst out in an angry stream.

"I just — I just hate it when he treats me like one of his witnesses!"

Her mother sighed an understanding sigh.

"I know," she answered quietly. "But he really doesn't mean to. It's just that he works all day and it takes a while for him to switch over from lawyer to father when he gets home."

"Well, it's not fair," Camden said, pouting.

"You're right," her mom agreed. "It isn't fair."

That seemed to help a little. Camden shrugged.

"I guess he gets stuck in the trial-mode and can't get out," she said.

Her mother chuckled. "I think you're right."

After a moment, she looked Camden straight in the eye.

"Honey, what is all this new slang you're bringing home?"

Camden tried to give her an honest answer.

"Just words," she mumbled.

Mrs. Douglas was trying to be nice about it.

"Well, it seems you use them on purpose just to make us angry."

"I do not!" Camden protested. "I just get stuck in that mode too, like Dad. And it's hard for me to switch over the minute I get home!"

Her mom raised an eyebrow. "It's hardly the same thing, Camden."

"It *is* the same thing, Mom," she insisted. "What's the difference? Just because he's the father, he gets a special deal?"

Her mother smiled. "Well, yes, I guess he does."

"And I don't?" Camden asked.

"We give you special understanding, Camden. Your father sent me up here to talk to you for just that reason."

This time Camden raised the eyebrow.

"And he couldn't come himself?" She hugged her pillow.

Her mother sighed.

"He sent me because he was angry, and he didn't want to take it out on you. Now don't you think you owe him an apology?" she asked.

Camden could tell that this was very important to her mother, so she gave in.

"Okay, I'll tell him I'm sorry, Mom," she said. "But why can't he ever apologize once in a while?"

Her mother shrugged. "I don't know, honey," she said softly, stroking Camden's arm.

Why do mothers always have to be touching kids? wondered Camden. But she didn't take her arm away.

They sat without talking for a while. Finally Mrs. Douglas stood up.

"You think you guys have it tough," she said. "I have to switch from mother to wife and later on to teacher. You're not going to believe this, but sometimes cook seems the easiest."

Camden laughed.

Her mother couldn't resist the impulse to hug her.

"I love you, honey," she whispered into Camden's blonde hair and left the room.

Mothers always have to be saying that, too, she thought. But the bruise inside felt better.

15

Word Police

THE LAST THING Camden wanted to do that night was dream the planet dream. She was more in the mood for a nice, warm, cuddly dream — maybe with kittens. Instead she found herself flying across the vastness, riding high on the Star Wind. She breezed past a fuzzy cluster of light that seemed to be a single hazy cloud hanging all alone in space. She saw a group of stars streaking toward one another in a great circle. She felt sure they were going to crash, but at the moment before impact, they stopped dead. Then the stars twirled and turned together as though they were playing in a child's circle dance. The circle spun one way, then the other, faster and faster. Finally the stars flew away in a follow-the-leader streak of light.

Well, thought Camden, I guess stars can have fun, too.

Sooner than she'd hoped, Camden spotted the familiar bronze sun and began her descent toward the small, troubled world. The dream didn't waste any time once it had landed her planetside. She was guided quickly through the bronze glowing streets toward the Great Hall of Learning.

"I don't really feel like going back there," she said to the dream. Nonetheless, she was taken right up to the steps of the dark tower, where a large crowd of bronze-haired people had gathered. Camden noticed a lot of pushing and shoving among the people as she glided smoothly through the masses toward the front of the crowd.

Again Camden had the feeling that she was watching a silent film. She saw guards lining the front of the building to hold the people back. When Camden crept closer to see what it was that the guards were guarding, she could hardly believe it. As far as she could tell, they were protecting long lists of words!

The words were arranged in alphabetical order on long, thin sheets of bronze paper that clung to the black glass of the huge building. The guards were allowing one person at a time to approach. Each person seemed to be comparing something he had on the paper to the lists of words. And every last one of them turned away in defeat. Camden watched at least twelve pairs of shoulders slump in despair as the searchers found words they didn't want to see already written on the long lists.

Finally a very old woman with gray streaks in her bronze hair struggled to climb the steps. She teetered on the edge of the top step for a moment, but one of the guards prodded her forward. The little woman fumbled to find her glasses, scrunching up her nose to keep them in place. Then she uncrumpled her scrap of paper with a tiny word scrawled on it and held out an old, shaking finger to trace slowly down the list. The crowd had no patience, and soon Camden could see them begin to hoot and yell at her. This only made the old woman's face scrunch up tighter. Her finger crept at a snail's pace down the list, word by slow word.

After she had completed several pages, however, the crowd began to calm down. Camden could feel the tension in the air. The crowd seemed to suck in its breath as the old woman neared the bottom of the final page. When her shaking finger crept past the last word, the crowd went wild. They jumped up and down, threw hats in the air, and hugged one another in celebration of the little lady's victory. Her crinkled eyes opened wide and her face lit up with such delight that the crow's feet flew away and all her wrinkles seemed to disappear. Just for a moment, Camden caught a glimpse of the very beautiful young woman she must have been long ago.

The old woman laughed and danced a little jig, waving her paper in the face of the guards. They had no choice but to open the heavy glass doors and allow her to enter the Great Hall of Learning. She scurried quickly through them, waving to the crowd. Camden had just enough time to slip in behind her before the doors slammed shut.

Inside the hall, Camden followed the old woman as she almost skipped down the corridor. Once in a while, she would uncrumple her scrap of paper and look at the word again, as if to make sure it was still there. Camden chuckled as she followed her.

Without warning, a shadowy figure suddenly leaped out of a dark side corridor and grabbed the old lady.

"Nooooooooo!" Camden yelled.

She tried to run and stop him as the large man struggled with the frail old woman. But Camden's legs were sandbags and she seemed to be moving in slow motion. The man grabbed the paper out of the woman's hand. Then, without mercy, he knocked her to the ground. Camden tried to grab at him as he ran, but he seemed to pass right through her. He streaked down the hall to turn quickly and dash through a door that was marked WORD PAYMENTS.

When Camden turned back to her, the old lady was still lying in a crumpled heap on the floor. She didn't even try to get up. The tired old woman just lay there, beating her wrinkled fists against the ground. Camden tried to call for help, but it was only a dream and she couldn't make a sound. Helpless, she sank down next to the old woman to watch over her until someone came. Camden hugged her knees as tears splashed down her face, making puddles beside her on the floor of a dream.

But suddenly the dream urgently swept her up, forcing Camden to leave the defeated old woman behind. She was pulled out of the Great Hall and through the unhappy crowd. Camden sped past bronze buildings and down empty glowing avenues, faster and faster. She felt an urgency in the dream, as if she were running out of time.

Camden was turned quickly to the left down a side street; then she jogged to the right and found herself in the darkness of a dead-end alley. Camden peered around her. Far back, hidden in the shadows, she could see a very big, greasy-looking man, bronze hair slicked straight back. He was standing behind two long tables piled high with food and clothing. He was surrounded by two even larger guards with gruff faces and very gruff-looking guns.

Then Camden noticed a nervous husband and his wife huddled before them. She could tell that the man and the husband were arguing heavily even though she could hear nothing. The wife pulled a large bag from beneath her coat and laid out several freshly baked loaves of bread on the table. After giving them each a good poke with his dirty finger, the greasy man made an offer. More argument. Camden couldn't quite figure out what was going on. She thought the couple was going to buy food or clothing from the big man. But it appeared that they were giving him the bread instead.

Hmmmmmm, Camden mused, then the slimy guy must be selling something else in exchange for the woman's bread. What could he be selling that these people would be willing to give up their food for? And what could he be selling that has to be hidden away deep in the corner of a dark alley?

The argument was brought to an end quickly when the husband angrily pulled off his overcoat and threw it down on top of the bread as additional payment. Smiling, the huge man nodded to the guards, who went into the shabby building behind them.

Camden still couldn't figure out what was going on. She saw the couple turn their heads suddenly toward a window in the building. Troubled, they both quickly looked away again. Then one of the guards returned, rubbing his knuckles. He handed a small, stained piece of paper to the greasy one, who smiled again to reveal gray, broken teeth. When he reached over to give the paper to the husband, Camden finally put it all together.

The black market! she thought. These people are selling their bread for a word!

Once again, the husband and wife turned frightened eyes toward the building and Camden saw a terrified face appear at the window. His shirt torn, spectacles broken and hanging off one ear, the hostage tried to cry out to the people below. But a large, dirty hand quickly grabbed his face and pulled him out of Camden's sight.

The woman's face went white. Her husband looked ill and seemed to totter on the edge of a choice. Camden didn't move, waiting to see what he would do. Would he help the prisoner or would he take the paper and run? The black marketeer thrust the scrap toward him. But the husband was frozen. He stared at it with glazed eyes. Time seemed to hold its breath.

Suddenly the husband reached out and snatched the paper. Then he pulled his wife away from the dark alley, away from the guilt that was already beginning to eat at his heart.

Camden shook her head.

"I don't understand! I don't understand!" she mumbled as her dream stole her up and away from the dead-end alley.

"What is happening here?" she demanded of the dream. "This whole world has gone crazy!"

She couldn't shake the image of that tortured face in the window, unable even to cry out for help. And she couldn't shake the terrible feeling of not being able to do anything about it.

The dream took Camden out of the bronze city and into a quiet neighborhood area that looked familiar. When she arrived at a darkened house at the end of the block, Camden remembered it as the secret meeting place that she'd visited in an earlier dream.

She was whisked through the front door, down the hall, and up through the secret trap door. Once inside the stuffy attic room, Camden noticed many familiar faces. However, these faces were much thinner and very weary. The professor was at the head of the table, his crumpled hat by his side. The young teacher sat beside him, looking as if she could hardly keep her eyes open. On the other side of the table, Camden saw the large man with the gruff voice. He had several bandages on his face and a very nasty bruise under one eye.

As Camden entered, the sound kicked in. The professor was speaking again.

"So, it's decided," he announced. "We'll storm the Hall of Learning at the next full moon. We'll stop this word taxation and put that insane woman on trial in front of a jury of her peers!"

"That all sounds very simple," a man said from the back. He was tall with dark, heavy features hidden behind a brown hat. Camden didn't remember him from the first dream. "But you've forgotten that she has the Word Police and the Word Police have guns," he continued.

"We have guns too!" the young teacher responded. "We've been building a secret supply of arms all ready to take up against them."

But the professor shook his head angrily.

"We'll use the guns only to defend ourselves!" he said loudly. "Do you understand that, everyone?" he asked the group, pounding on the table. "Only in self-defense!"

The man in the back spoke up again.

"But how will so few be able to overpower so many?" he prodded.

"There are many, many more of us than you see here," the woman answered. "Each one of us here tonight represents friends, family, and neighbors. We are all prepared to do what we have to in order to stop this insanity."

"You don't understand what I'm trying to say," the man said. "People will die! Do you understand that? Are the lives of your family and friends worth it?"

"Is living without fear worth it?" The little professor stood up. "Look at us. Look at what we've become! No one sleeps anymore. We are forced to spend endless nights searching for some new word that hasn't yet been paid to the Tax. We live in fear of being dragged off to prison by the Word Police. And those of us who are teachers live in double fear, fear that we'll be taken by the black marketeers."

"That's right!" the woman agreed. "They steal us away in the night. Librarians, English professors, writers, poets, even kindergarten teachers! We live in terror that we'll be taken and the words forced out of us to sell on the black market!"

The image of that terrified man in the alley window flashed across Camden's mind.

The big man's rough voice rang out loudly.

"Our wives and our husbands are in prison. Children can no longer go to school. We have no more books or magazines or newspapers. She's taken them all. Do you know that there are actually thieves and robbers who specialize in stealing words? — *words*, for God's sake!"

Camden thought of the old woman beaten to the floor by a word thief.

"Yes," the young teacher said softly. "I think the cost that some of us will have to pay is equal to the price of freedom."

The man with the hat put on his overcoat.

"You're all fools," he stated. He climbed down through the trap door and slammed it behind him.

The room became silent.

"How have we come to this?" a woman asked. "How did this ever happen to us?"

"It's simple," the professor answered, sitting down again. "We elected someone who believed that learning should be painful. She took the joy out of it when she used reading and writing as methods of punishment. We should have impeached her when she sentenced that first criminal to five years of hard homework. But we didn't, and now learning has become torture. A poem is no longer beautiful when it is used to pay taxes. A word means nothing when it costs five apples and two heads of lettuce." He sighed. "We came to this because we didn't care enough to refuse and now it's too late."

"It's *not* too late!" someone yelled. "We'll storm the Hall of Learning!"

"An end to the Word Tax!" another added.

"An end to the Word Police!"

They worked themselves into such a frenzy that the small attic room seemed barely able to contain them. At that moment, Camden again felt that sudden sense of urgency from her dream. She was swept down through the trap door, out of the house, and onto the porch. There she saw the man with the hat who had stormed out earlier. He stood on the porch, waving a flashlight toward a row of houses across the street.

What's he doing? she wondered. And then Camden felt a stab of fear as she realized this must be a signal.

"Traitor!" she yelled at him.

The next instant, her dream caught her up and sped her across the street, close enough to see into the windows. A few quick glimpses of heavy, dark uniforms, stern faces, and guns told her everything she needed to know.

Camden drew in her breath.

"The Word Police," she whispered.

Then the dream twirled her around and she fairly flew back to the dark house. She flashed past the traitor on the porch, down the hall, and through the trap door.

They were still arguing. Camden found the professor.

"The Word Police!" she yelled. "The Word Police! They're coming!"

He went right on talking to the young woman.

"What's the matter with you?" Camden demanded. "Don't you understand?"

No response. He didn't seem to care. Camden tried to grab the professor's arm, but her hand passed right through him as if she weren't even there.

Oh no! she thought, finally realizing that he couldn't hear her. She had forgotten that she couldn't make a sound.

Frantic, Camden tried to break through the dream anyway.

"Run! Run!" she yelled. But they went right on arguing. "The Word Police! Run!" she cried.

Camden yelled until her lungs burned and her throat felt like sandpaper. It was no use. She finally gave up, slumping helplessly in a corner. She was forced to watch as the Word Police broke through the trap door. She saw the brave rebels fight them with chairs, sticks, brooms, even fists. But she could do nothing except be a witness to their capture.

"I'm sorry," she said as she watched them being prodded with guns and loaded into paddy wagons to be taken to who-knows-what awful place.

"I'm so sorry," she repeated one last time as the Star Wind lifted her up into the blessed silence of space.

16

Life Is the Pits

M_{AW}?"

Camden woke up with a start, staring straight into the eyes of her cat.

"Maw?" Maggie asked again, laying a concerned paw on Camden's arm.

"Oh, Maggie, what a nightmare!" Camden shook her head and sat up. "That was an official, honest-to-goodness nightmare, nothing fun about it."

Maggie knew how scary those could be.

"It was just awful," Camden said, shaking her head again to clear it. "I can't even talk about it, it was so bad."

That was fine with Maggie. She probably didn't want to hear about it anyway. She just wanted to make sure Camden was all right.

"I'm fine. I'm fine, Maggie. Go back to sleep now. Really, I'm just fine."

Maggie took her at her word and curled up again. But Camden had lied. She wasn't just fine at all; she felt terrible. She couldn't figure out why she cared so much, though. It wasn't as if the rebels or the Word Police were real or anything. They were only made-up dream people. They didn't exist in her world, just as she didn't exist in theirs. So why did she still feel so awful? The bad feelings were supposed to stay in the dream. But she couldn't make them go away.

For no particular reason, out of nowhere, Camden began to think about *The Jungle Books*. She wondered about the wolf boy, his friend the bear, and the black panther. She began to have a strange desire to see how they were doing.

Good, she thought. Maybe they can help me forget about the planet dream.

She reached over to her bedside table, but the book wasn't there.

Hmmmm, now where did it go? she wondered. Leaning over to feel around on the floor, Camden found the book shoved under the bed. She blew off the fine film of dust that had collected on its cover, feeling a twinge of guilt.

"Sorry I haven't finished you yet," she said to the book. "No excuses."

Camden thought she might try to finish it that night, so she could tell her dad the next morning.

"Get him off my back," she mumbled to herself.

But she couldn't find her place. Thumbing through the book, she tried to remember where she had left off. Nothing looked familiar. She remembered the boy who grew up with a wolf pack, but she couldn't bring the names to mind. The words didn't make sense either. The writing looked like a huge jumbled mess of words and letters. It was so confusing, she got angry and threw the book back on the floor.

"And you can just stay there and rot for all I care!" she yelled at it. "You're a double ungood grownie thing, that's all you are!"

Camden threw the covers over her head to pout.

Maggie opened one eye. She thought Camden was being just a little childish.

"You're right," Camden answered from under the pile of blankets. "What am I doing?"

Maggie had no idea.

"Why am I acting like such a baby?" she asked, pulling the covers off her head. "This is double ungood."

Her cat agreed.

Camden couldn't understand where these sudden bursts of temper were coming from.

"Am I going crazy?" she asked.

Maggie thought it might be possible.

Camden grabbed her pillow. "Well, there's really no reason at all except that my life is the pits," she said. "My dad takes everything out on me and my mom lets him. My friends only care about WT-3. They make fun when I forget to speak The Words. Every time I go to sleep I have this terrible dream, and now I can't even read an old book! Aside from that, I'm having a wonderful time!"

Maggie thought Camden was just feeling sorry for herself and went back to sleep.

Camden pouted again.

"And now my very own cat doesn't even care!"

She was so depressed, she went down to the kitchen to make a peanut butter sandwich.

17

Spaghetti Sauce

MITCH? Is that Mitch?" Mrs. Douglas called from the kitchen. Camden and her friend were trying to sneak out the front door without being noticed.

"Don't you dare leave without coming in here and saying hello!" she called.

Mitch was friends with Camden's mom. They often sat around having long talks about books. She even brought books home from the high school library for him. They *used* to be friends anyway, before the summer and WT-3. Now it was a battle for Camden to get him to come into the house.

He rolled his eyes.

"C'mon, Mitch," she whispered. "Just say hello. It'll only take a second. Besides, I have to ask if I can go to WT-3's."

Groaning, he followed her into the kitchen.

"Hi, Mitch," Mrs. Douglas said as she put raw spaghetti into a pot of boiling water. "It's about time you got in here."

He gave her a fast smile and a quick nod.

"Mom," Camden asked, "don't you think spaghetti is a little weird for breakfast?"

"Yes," she answered. "But this isn't breakfast, it's dinner."

"Mom." Camden tried to be gentle. "It's ten o'clock in the morning."

"I know," her mother answered. "But I'm cooking the entire meal tonight and I thought I'd get a head start just in case it doesn't turn out."

She tasted a spoonful of spaghetti sauce and considered it for a moment. Then she dipped another spoonful and carried it over to Mitch.

"Tell me the truth. Don't be afraid to hurt my feelings," she told him. "I just want to know, should I throw it out and start all over?"

Mitch shook his head.

"Pass," he mumbled.

"Just a little taste, Mitch," she pleaded. "I need your help here."

But Mitch crossed his arms and shook his head again, frowning at her.

"Please!" she said, laughing, as she brought the spoon close up to his clenched lips.

"Double pass!" he shouted at her and shoved the spoon away, spilling sauce all over the floor.

Mrs. Douglas looked at him in surprise, her carefree mood destroyed. Camden reached for a towel and quickly cleaned the mess up.

"Okay, okay," her mother said quietly. "You don't have to taste it. Sorry I asked."

"I'll taste it, Mom." Camden grabbed a spoon and swallowed a mouthful of sauce. "Mmmmmmmmmm, great! Perfecto!" she said, throwing a death glare at Mitch.

Mrs. Douglas reached into the refrigerator without saying a word. Mitch let out a loud, bored sigh and tapped his foot.

"So, Mom," Camden said, trying to change the subject, "we thought we'd mosey on down to Venice today, if that's all right with you."

"Venice?" Her mother looked up. "Didn't you go down there one day last week?"

"Yes," Camden muttered. Actually, she had been four or five times, but her mom didn't know that.

Mrs. Douglas turned to Mitch, who was now leaning against the door looking as bored as possible, humming to himself.

"What is it with that place?" she asked him. "Why don't you kids go to the beach, or roller-skating, or swimming in your pool? I'd even settle for video games!"

"We do," he answered.

"Just one or all of the above?" she asked, challenge in the air.

He sighed and explained slowly as if he were talking to a five-year-old. "The Kidsters hang down with the sand lizards."

Tensing her lips, Mrs. Douglas spoke in her formal teacher's tone. "Excuse me?" she asked.

"Uh, uh, he means we do go to the beach, Mom," Camden piped up, shooting another glare at Mitch. He knew better than to use The Words in front of her parents. But he just shrugged and kept tapping his foot.

Mrs. Douglas laughed.

"Boy, you two must think you're dealing with a nincompoop here. C'mon, what do you really do down at this friend's house all day? I know you don't go to the beach; you're both about as tan as this guy."

She held up the wet raw chicken that she was washing in the sink.

"Tans are for sand lizards," Mitch answered. "Rollerskating is a no-go. The pool is full of my grownie brothers and video games cause brain-drain."

"I see," she answered. "Then what do you do, if I may ask?"

"What we do," he said scornfully, "is the great escape from Grownieville where we don't have to ask permission every time we want to cross the street!"

Mrs. Douglas's eyes widened and Camden groaned out loud.

"Mr. Malkovich," she said stiffly. "If I really wanted to hear that kind of rudeness in my own home, I would simply invite all of my students here."

"Do I care?" He shrugged.

"However," she continued, "since I don't hold open house for my classes, I think it's clear that I expect a certain amount of politeness from my guests."

He started to speak but she held her hand up to cut him off.

"Unless that's an apology, I don't want to hear another

word out of your mouth. And since you don't seem to be able to respect my home, I assume that you no longer wish to be considered a guest." She stared at him.

Camden had heard this hyper-polite attitude from her mother before. It always meant that Camden was in deep trouble.

Mitch stared right back at Mrs. Douglas but didn't say anything.

"Apparently I haven't made myself clear, young man!" she continued. "You are no longer a guest in this house!"

Mitch started to speak but thought better of it. He turned on his heel and stormed out without a word. Mrs. Douglas turned to Camden.

"What is the matter with you kids?" she demanded. "I can't believe that was Mitch. It's as though he's not even the same person!"

Camden didn't know what to say. Her mother was right, however. Mitch wasn't the same as he used to be. Her mom sighed heavily, and for a frightening moment Camden thought she was going to cry.

"I used to like him," she said softly and turned back to the sink.

For a fleeting instant, Camden saw her mother in a different light. She saw her as a girl, just like herself, who'd lost a friend. Camden knew the feeling.

"Just what was that all about, Mitch?"

Camden stood in front of his bike, hands on her hips, blocking his way.

"So I laid a little of The Words on your mom, no big," he answered, trying to steer his front wheel around her. She grabbed the handlebars angrily.

"You know my grownies go into the mad-mode double quick with slang. You did it on purpose!" she yelled at him.

He twirled the pedal with his foot. "She's a grownie. What can I say?"

Camden shook the handlebars. "Well, she was just trying to be nice and you hurt her feelings!"

He snorted, jerking the handlebars out of her grasp.

"Who cares about grownie feelings? Trash 'em!"

But Camden didn't consider her mom just any old grownie.

"She's not so bad," she said.

Mitch raised an eyebrow. "You're not talking like a Kidster, CD-1."

This made Camden angry all over again.

"I'm just as much a Kidster as you are!" she answered between her teeth. "Just don't be rude to my mom anymore, got it?"

They locked eyes for a long minute.

"WT won't like this, CD-1," he said slowly.

This sounded much too close to a threat for Camden's liking.

"Oh? What are you going to do, Mitch? Tell on me? I'm not afraid of WT the way you are!"

"I'm not afraid of him!" he yelled at her angrily.

"Are too."

"Am not!"

"Are too!"

He squinted at her. "WT won't let you play The Game anymore, CD-1."

She glared at him. "What do you mean?" Camden suddenly felt that uncomfortable craving again.

"If you think like a double ungood grownie and you act like one and talk like one, then WT won't let you play The Game anymore," he answered in a superior tone.

"Will too!" she retorted.

"Will not."

"Will too!"

"Will not!"

Furious, she shoved at his bike, almost toppling him over.

"Who do you think you are, Mitch Malkovich? I can play The Game if I want to and nobody's going to stop me!"

"WT will," he answered with a cruelty in his voice that Camden had never heard before. Then he pulled his bike away and rode off alone.

Camden watched him ride down the street.

Boy, life can really be the pits, she thought. What did he mean by that? Why can't I play The Game anymore?

Camden didn't know what she'd do without The Game. She really didn't want to think about it.

"Maggie!" she called. Camden needed a friendly face. But there was no answer as she slumped down onto the porch steps.

Who does he think he is, telling me I can't play? she

asked herself. "Great, now I've lost my best friend," she added aloud. And life didn't look too good without a best friend.

"Maggie!" Camden called again. No response. "Well, I'm going to WT's," she announced and went to get her bike. By the time Maggie bounded around the corner in answer to her call, Camden was already on her way to Venice.

18

No-Go

WHEN SHE ARRIVED at the (Something) View Arms, Camden marched boldly into the hotel lobby. She found the Kidsters in their usual places on the floor around WT-3. When she slipped into an empty spot next to Dan, Mitch gave her a dirty look. WT was in the middle of another speech.

"Grownies are afraid of Kidster minds," he told them. "They force us into their prison-schools to shove their grownie words into our heads."

The Kidsters agreed.

"All grownies are double ungood and everything they do is a double badness for Kidsters," he went on. "Their rules and reasons and permissions cause brain-drain. Don't listen to them! Turn your backs on the grownie world!"

Camden thought about the way Mitch had treated her mother and she decided she'd had just about enough of this.

"WT-3!" she interrupted. "I don't think all grownies are a badness. They just get stuck in the grownie-mode and can't get out. It's not their fault."

The Kidsters turned to stare at her with shocked faces.

WT frowned. "Everything is their fault," he said.

"No, it's not!" Camden answered bravely. She'd show Mitch she wasn't afraid of this guy. "They just have a lot of stuff to do all the time and it makes them mondo-crazed. I mean, I think The Words are really cosmic and everything, but why do we have to hate our parents?"

She looked over at Mitch but he avoided her gaze. The lobby rumbled with disapproval as the Kidsters whispered among themselves, wondering what WT was going to do.

In answer, he got up and walked slowly to where Camden was sitting. Boots crunching against the gritty floor, he walked around her like an animal sizing up its prey. He circled her once, then suddenly stopped directly behind her. Camden didn't move. When his voice rang out, she jumped.

"CD-1 is thinking un-Kidster!" he announced. "She's been hanging with her grownies too double much. Looks like CD-1 and The Words are a no-go, looks like CD-1 and The Game are a no-go!"

"Wait a second!" Camden protested, twisting around to look at him. "I still want to play The Game and do The Words!"

"Looks like CD-1 is too close to grownieness," he continued, ignoring her. "She's been sent by them to wreck the Kidsters, to make us mondo-crazed with her grownie ways!"

Hank leaped to his feet, malice in his eye.

"Double right, WT!" he said. "She's come to trash the Kidsters. She's always nose-poking around. I even saw her on the secret stairway!" His pointed finger accused her. "She was trying to break down the door-unit!"

The entire group sucked in its breath.

He saw me! Camden thought.

Then she felt two very strong, angry hands grip her shoulders. WT twirled her around to face him and the fire in his eyes shot right through her.

"Is this a trueness?" he demanded, gripping her shoulders painfully. She tried to wriggle out of his grasp but he held her tight. Camden gulped, thinking fast. She had no idea how to get out of this mess.

"Well, I wasn't exactly trying to break it down," she finally admitted. His hands gripped more tightly. "I was just curious. Besides, why does it have to be such a big deal? Why is it such a secret? Are you hiding something in there that you don't want us to see?"

WT angrily jerked Camden to her feet, forcing her to stand before the Kidsters as if she were on trial.

"CD-1 thinks grownie. She talks grownie and she nose-pokes where no good Kidster should. CD-1 is a double badness," he announced. "And I say we do a pass on her unit! I say CD-1 is a no-go!"

"She's a no-go!" Hank eagerly agreed.

"A no-go!" Mark said.

"No-go," Nancy added.

One by one, Camden's friends rejected her. Mitch was the last one to vote. He looked at WT, then back to Camden. She held her breath. Everything would be all right if Mitch was still on her side.

"MM-3?" WT prodded.

Mitch let his eyes drop for a moment and Camden could tell he was fighting some kind of internal battle. He glanced up, and for a fleeting instant Camden thought she could see an apology in his eyes. Then his face hardened and he turned away.

"No-go!" he said harshly.

Camden felt as though someone had slapped her across the face. She couldn't believe that Mitch, too, had turned against her. She knew he was mad at her, but she didn't think he was *that* mad. Her shoulders slumped and she grabbed her backpack. No one would look at her as she walked slowly across the dingy lobby. At the door she turned back to them for a moment.

"Double-bye," she called softly and left the hotel.

Riding home with the wind blowing against her face, Camden tried to sort the whole mess out. How did that happen? she wondered. I guess I'd been thinking those things for a long time and I finally got mad enough to say it. But now I'm kicked out, so I'll never play The Game again and I'll never learn The Words, and now I have no friends. That was a tough one. What was she going to do when school started and she would have to see the Kidsters every day? What would she do when they made fun of her with The Words? No friends, that was like a death sentence. Maybe she could convince her parents to move to another town.

The worst part about it was Mitch's betrayal. How could he do that to his best friend? He told me what would happen if I stuck up for grownies in front of WT-3, she recalled. Maybe that was some kind of warning. I wonder if he knew I would get kicked out. It was all so confusing and that uncomfortable craving was back. She groaned and pedaled faster.

When Camden finally rode up to her house, she found Maggie sitting on the front steps. Her white paws folded neatly, she was waiting patiently for her friend to return. Camden picked up her cat.

"Maggie," she said, nuzzling her fur, "it's you and me and nobody else."

Maggie had thought so all along.

That night Camden's mother fixed a great dinner. Camden didn't see any sign of the spaghetti she'd been cooking earlier. She decided not to ask. After her father watched her pick at her chicken and push her potatoes around the plate, he asked if anything was wrong.

"What?" Camden looked up, not sure if she had been spoken to.

"Are you feeling all right, Cammie?" he asked. "You look as though you've had a hard day at the office."

Camden offered a half-smile.

"No, I'm okay," she answered. "I just —" She broke off, shrugging her shoulders.

Her mother thought Camden's mood might have come from the argument with Mitch that morning.

"It's okay about Mitch," she told her daughter. "I was just surprised at his attitude."

Camden tried to swallow the carrot she'd been struggling

with for the last five minutes. She was trying very hard not to cry. But she didn't think she would make it.

"May I be excused? I'm really not hungry," she mumbled, and before they could reply she ran upstairs to her room.

Throwing herself onto her bed, Camden grabbed her pillow, but the tears didn't come. She lay very still, thinking about how miserable her life was going to be without friends.

"Cammie?" It was her dad. He knocked softly. "Cammie, may I come in?"

Camden moaned silently. She just wanted to be left alone.

"I'm real tired, Dad. I think I'm just going to go to bed now, if that's okay," she said to the door.

"It won't take long," he answered. "I just want to talk to you for a little bit."

He opened the door, peeking his head around.

"Okay?" he asked.

Do I have a choice? she thought to herself.

"Oh, okay," she said and sat up, putting her pillow aside.

Her father stepped in and glanced nervously around. Camden couldn't remember the last time he had been in her room.

"What's this?" he asked, picking a book up off the floor. It was *The Jungle Books*, still lying against the wall where she'd thrown it. He bent the cover back into place.

Oh, great, Camden thought. All I need right now is for him to start yelling about some dumb book.

But her father simply sat down next to her on the bed and cleared his throat.

"Camden," he said. "I know I've been hard on you lately. It's just that I'm under a lot of pressure with this trial and —"

"What with the trial?" she interrupted.

"Pressure," he repeated.

"Oh," she replied, but she really didn't know what he meant.

"And I just can't handle a lot of problems at home right now," he told her.

Camden squirmed. This whole thing was making her uncomfortable.

"It's okay, Dad," she answered. "That's not why I was in a bad mood anyway."

"Do you want to talk about it?" he asked.

"Well, no, it's not that big a thing. I just lost all of my friends today." She laughed, trying to make light of it.

"What do you mean?" he asked.

"I mean, I have no friends! I've been fired from my peer group." Camden pulled at the threads on her bedspread.

"What happened?" he asked.

"Well" — she shrugged — "I guess it was because I happened to disagree with WT . . . uh, I mean this one guy, about some things, and they kicked me out."

Her father frowned. "What is he — the president of the club or something?"

Camden sighed. "Yeah, I guess you could call him that."

He patted her arm. "Well, whatever the reason, Camden, I'm proud of you for standing up to this guy."

He got to his feet.

"Besides," he continued, "they probably weren't the kind

of people you wanted as friends anyway."

Parents *always* say that, Camden thought to herself.

"Well, thanks for putting up with my temper lately," he said. "Things will be easier after this trial. Now I'd better go help your mother with the dishes before she kicks *me* out."

"Bye, Dad." Camden managed a smile.

She waited until he had gone before grabbing her pillow again. Her father had made her feel better. At least he admitted that he's been mean to me, she thought. I wouldn't exactly call that an apology — she hugged her pillow tight — but I guess it's close enough.

19

"Sorry, Mr. Kipling"

Iₙ ʜᴇʀ ᴅʀᴇᴀᴍs late that night, the Star Wind blew through her window and swept Camden away into the twinkling darkness. Flying free, twirling and spinning with endless speed, she couldn't hold back the feeling of joy that rode with her like a friend through the night.

This is better than that stupid Game any day, she thought.

Soon Camden located the flaming bronze sun among the sparkling stars and began to descend toward the tiny world.

It was night on the bronze planet. The dream guided her through gloomy streets; she noticed that their bronze glow had disappeared. Primitive torches broke the dark with a flickering light.

But there were people everywhere, all out in the streets. Camden thought there must be hundreds of people. They stood very still in huddled groups or sat on curbs and stairs or wandered around aimlessly with nowhere to go and nothing to do. There was an empty look in their eyes, as if they had forgotten who they were or where they lived. Camden shuddered. Something was very wrong here.

She looked out across the square and saw hundreds more of the same lifeless faces as her dream guided her up the steps of the Great Hall of Learning. In the faces of all of them Camden could see a great sadness, as if they had lost something very dear to them. She slipped past the Word Police and through the huge black doors.

Inside, the immense hall was deserted. Camden's dream turned her around and down a flight of dark, damp steps that spiraled deep under the Great Hall. She finally reached the bottom and looked out onto a long row of barred doors.

This must be where they keep the prisoners, she thought.

Camden's dream guided her slowly past door after barred door until she stopped at the very last one on the end. She thought she could hear muffled voices as the dream passed her through the door and into the dark cell inside. There she found some old friends.

The young woman was slumped against a splintered wooden cot, shivering from the cold. She was dressed in the same torn, dirty clothes that she had been wearing the night of the Word Police's raid. When she looked up, Camden could see dark circles of fatigue under her eyes. Across from her, leaning against the damp stone wall, the large, bearlike man muttered angrily to himself. One of his arms was hanging in a homemade sling and a torn rag served as a bandage for his head.

"Professor." The man's rough voice sounded as if he hadn't slept for a month. "Professor," he repeated.

A very thin, old gentleman with gray hair and a white beard turned to face his fellow prisoners. He hobbled toward them, supporting himself with a cane. Camden wouldn't have recognized him at all had it not been for the very tattered brown hat on his head.

"He's grown so old," she whispered to herself.

The professor had an exhausted, battered look, as if he'd been fighting a long battle that he knew he could never win.

"Professor," the man continued, "you can't go on."

"You're getting weaker and weaker every day," the young woman added. "If you give her what she wants, they'll let you out of here."

But the professor shook his head, coughing violently.

"You have to have some decent food and a warm, dry place," she urged. "You have to have your strength to fight."

He looked at them with a puzzled expression.

"Fight for what?" he croaked in a ragged voice. "If I give her what she wants, there won't be anything left to fight for."

"She's going to get it anyway," the man added somberly, "one way or another. She'll take what she wants."

Easing himself onto the cot, the old professor chuckled softly.

"Then I have to refuse," he answered simply. "Don't you see? We're the last ones left. And she wants it all. The poetry and plays, the speeches, the sonnets and short stories. Every novel, every lyric, every song and ballad!" His voice cracked with strain. "Everything we've ever read or studied or written or remembered. All of it!" He paused, gasping for breath. "And when she's stolen it all, every single word," he continued softly, "then the last flickering candle will be snuffed out and that will be the end of thought."

There was a long silence before the man slammed his fist against the wall angrily.

"No! We can write them!" he declared. "Write down all the words we remember!"

The woman shrugged her thin shoulders.

"Try it," she said.

Digging quickly into his pockets for a pen or pencil, the man came up with nothing. But she reached down into the side of her ragged shoe and emerged with a pathetic stub of a pencil. She handed it to him carefully.

The man grabbed the stub, then searched frantically for something to write his words down on. But there wasn't a shred of anything resembling paper in the cell. Finally, in desperation, he turned and planted his pencil stub against the wall, ready to write every single word he ever knew right there on the cold stone.

But nothing happened. The woman crossed her arms knowingly while the professor dropped his gray head into his hands. Camden waited.

The man grunted and tried again, but the pencil didn't budge. He frowned and strained until Camden thought his head would explode, but the pencil stayed right where it was. He sucked in a great breath of air and tried one last time. Camden could see the point of the pencil bite deep into the stone with his effort, but it didn't move at all.

With a yell of rage, the man threw the pencil onto the floor and stomped on it, grinding it out with his shoe. Then he slumped down in a corner, and Camden could see that the pencil stub had been crushed into a fine powder that would soon mix with the dust of the prison cell as if it had never written a word.

She decided it was time to wake up. All of this was just too painful to watch. She felt so helpless and she couldn't stand to see the professor looking so tired and defeated.

"Can we go now?" she asked her dream irritably. "I don't know why you brought me here. There's nothing I can do!"

And before she knew it, Camden was flying free among the stars, speeding on the Star Wind home.

Camden opened her eyes and yawned.

"Boy," she muttered. "What a rotten dream that turned out to be."

She didn't sleep any more that night. Tiptoeing softly past her parents' bedroom, Camden slipped silently down the stairs to the living room, where she could sit in her father's chair and think about things for a while.

It'd be awful living on the bronze planet, she thought. Those poor people. I guess the Teacher just took every word they ever knew. That's why they were all standing around like a bunch of zombies. They can't even talk to each other anymore. They'll never read a story again or hear a song. They probably can't even think! That is *really* the pits.

Suddenly Camden was hit with an overwhelming sense of urgency. She had to do something and fast. But what?

She couldn't think of anything that needed to be done. Yet the feeling refused to go away.

"I don't know what to do!" she complained aloud.

"Maw?"

"Maggie." Camden reached down to pet her cat as Maggie rubbed her back along the chair.

"I had that dream again, Maggie," Camden told her. "And the whole planet was a total mess. The Teacher had stolen all the words and the professor was in jail and the big man couldn't write anymore. I know it's just a dream and all, but I have this weird feeling that I should do something, only I don't know what!"

Maggie thought it was impossible to do anything about her dream except stop dreaming it. Maybe there was something that Camden could do here in real life.

She considered this. "Maybe you're right," she said. "You know, the thing that I really want to do more than anything else is read a book. Is that dumb? I mean, I'd like to read a book for the professor because he'll never be able to read one again."

Maggie licked a paw casually. She really didn't understand all this reading business, but if that was what Camden wanted to do . . .

"Oh, Maggie," she said, giggling, "you're such a cat sometimes."

Looking over her parents' extensive bookshelf, Camden pulled out *The Jungle Books*.

"Aha! Where have you been?" she asked, leafing through

the pages. The last thing she remembered was throwing the book down in disgust.

"Sorry, Mr. Kipling," she said. "I lost my head. Now where did I leave off?" she mumbled.

But she couldn't understand what it said. It looked as if it had been written in a different language. None of the words made any sense. She struggled to read it.

"Jumble, jumble, came to the . . . jumble something . . . went over — What is this?" she demanded. "I can't believe this is the same book I was reading at summer camp!"

Camden sat down again in her father's big armchair. Is it possible to forget how to read? she wondered. Maybe I'm just rusty because I haven't opened a book since . . . since . . . WT and all of that. How can I possibly have forgotten how to read?

She tried again on a different page but had the same problem.

"Something ran to the . . . something and . . . he something up —" Camden rubbed her hands over her face, staring straight ahead.

Visions of the planet dream flashed across her mind. The hundreds of empty faces, the young teacher slumped to the floor in despair, the large man snuffing out the pencil with his heel, the old professor with his head in his hands. And, once again, Camden was overcome by a feeling of time running out, of the need to do something right now!

Leaping up, she dashed over to her parents' dictionary,

which was so big it had its own special stand. She lifted it with both hands and carried the book back to her chair. Her legs almost buckling from the weight of it, she placed the huge old dictionary on her lap and picked up *The Jungle Books* again. Maggie was curled into a tight ball, fast asleep.

"Maggie," Camden called to her sternly, "wake up. This is important."

The cat opened her eyes and stretched. She knew a serious tone of voice when she heard one.

"Now," Camden announced, "it seems that I have completely forgotten how to read. I'm brain-drained. I don't know how this terrible thing could have happened. But nothing is going to stop me from learning all over again. Do you understand?"

Maggie understood.

"I'm going to start at the beginning of this book and I'm going to look up every single word I don't know in this, uh . . . this, uh . . ." She'd forgotten the word for it. "The thing that has all the words in it. Is that clear?" she asked Maggie.

It was clear.

Camden looked away and whispered, "I won't let myself end up like those planet people. I just won't."

Camden started from page one. She found that she knew some words but not others. She could still recognize little words like THE and ON and GO. But she couldn't get a lot of the important ones, the ones that told the story. There also didn't seem to be any rhyme or reason to which words she knew and which ones she didn't. Slowly, very slowly, Camden worked her way through the first page, then another and another. The letters and syllables were very confusing, but she sounded each one out aloud.

"I feel like a first grader," she grumbled.

It was even difficult to read the dictionary because she couldn't understand a lot of those words, either. As she finally figured out the meaning for each one, she felt as if a light had suddenly been switched back on in her brain. But it was very slow.

Word by word, Camden pressed on. But it was terribly difficult, and more than once she wanted to give up. Her head ached from the effort.

"When the moon rose over the plain," she read aloud slowly, ". . . making it look all milky, the . . . uh, hor . . . horri . . . horrified —" Camden's fingers scurried through the pages of the dictionary in a mad scramble to find the word.

"Horrified, horrify — here it is." When she read the meaning she almost laughed out loud. Of course! She knew what horrify meant. She had always known. How could she ever have been so dumb?

"Horrified vil . . . villa . . . villagers . . ."

Back to the dictionary to find VILLAGERS. And on and on. When she'd finished with a whole sentence, she read it aloud once more just to make sure.

"When the moon rose over the plain, making it look all

milky, the horrified villagers saw Mowgli, with two wolves at his heels and a bundle on his head, trotting across at the steady wolf's trot that eats up the miles like fire."

When Camden could finally understand an entire sentence, then the paragraphs began to mean something and then the whole page. Soon, like a runaway snowball building up speed, she was caught up in the world of Mowgli the wolf boy and his gray brothers.

Maggie stayed up the whole night watching over Camden. She never even yawned once.

In the morning Mr. Douglas found his daughter in the living room, sitting in his chair with the huge family dictionary in her lap. Her head was bent over the book as if she were studying it very carefully. But when he got closer, he saw that she was sound asleep, with her cat standing guard.

It took Camden weeks to work her way slowly through *The Jungle Books*. She read day and night, stopping only for meals, chores, and once in a while a bike ride. Her parents didn't know what to make of it. When they asked her about this sudden change, she told them not to worry.

"It's just a phase," she said with a wry grin.

During all that time, not one of Camden's friends stopped by to see how she was doing. She really hadn't expected them to. Once she tried calling Mitch just to see what he would say. But Mrs. Malkovich told her he wasn't at home, and he never called back. Camden missed her friends but there was nothing she could do about it. She certainly wasn't going to go crawling back to WT-3. Besides, she had a very important project and she found plenty of friends in her book.

After a while, Camden discovered that the painful bruise she had felt inside was gone. Perhaps the wrong hadn't been with her father after all.

20

The Power-Unit

CAMDEN DIDN'T DREAM about the bronze planet for a long time. She thought maybe she had seen the last of the old professor and his fellow rebels. She had to admit that she was a little relieved not to have to watch their suffering anymore. But another part of her missed all the people she had met in her dream. She felt as if they were her friends and now she didn't know what was happening to them. It was a little like switching off the television set right in the middle of a good movie.

But late one hot night near the end of summer, Camden found herself riding high on the Star Wind once again. She felt herself twirling around and up into the silent stillness of space. Soon she found the tiny bronze planet among the shining stars of the deep black night.

The dream didn't waste any time once Camden had landed planetside. She was whisked quickly past deserted streets, through the familiar black doors of the Hall of Learning, down the long winding stairs, and into the dark prison below.

I wonder how the old professor's doing, she thought. And, as if in reply, the dream swept her into the cold, damp cell.

Camden was shocked at how pale he was, pale and very weak. He was lying on the wooden cot, staring up at the stone ceiling. The thin young woman pulled her tattered shawl from her shoulders and laid it over the old man.

"Try to sleep," she murmured, casting a painful look at the big man, who was standing very still in the corner. He stared at the wall with vacant eyes.

Oh, no! Camden thought. He's like the others!

The young woman moved over to her friend and took him by the hand. He didn't resist as she led him to a pile of rags on the floor and helped him to sit down. She gazed at him sadly and placed a gentle hand on his cheek. There was no response, but then she probably hadn't expected any.

At the sound of a key in the rusty metal lock, the young woman stood up quickly, moving to the professor's side. He tried to push himself up on an elbow, but he didn't have the strength. Grabbing his hand tightly, the young woman faced the door with defiance as two Word Police stomped into the cell. They hauled her up roughly, tearing her hand out of the professor's frail grasp.

"Keep fighting, professor," she whispered, struggling vainly against the guards. But they held her easily between them as the heavy door was flung open and the Teacher strode into the room.

Camden cringed. She could feel the evil power emanating from this horrible creature, and it made her want to flee.

Terrified, Camden shrank back, making herself as tiny as possible against the wall. She was too afraid even to wake up.

The Teacher had changed since Camden first saw her so long ago in the Grand Classroom. Gone were the round spectacles, the simple dress. The Teacher now wore a black cape that floated around her as if it had a life of its own. She seemed larger than before and filled the tiny cell with a dark presence that sucked up the stale air.

And her eyes! They seemed to know everything! The Teacher's eyes were filled with an awesome knowledge, a cold, dark, secret knowledge that was wrong somehow. It was as if she had gained an understanding of the universe, then turned it, twisted it into something wicked. Camden shuddered. The Teacher knew things no one should ever know.

With long, spidery fingers the Teacher reached out to grab the frightened woman's face. Then, from deep within the flowing folds of her robe, she held up a small gray cube that spun wildly on its axis.

Camden rubbed at her eyes as the Teacher held the twirling vortex up in front of the young woman's face.

Camden bolted upright in her bed. Eyes wide, she stared straight ahead into the darkness of her room.

"I can't believe it," she whispered in shock. "WT . . . WT's power-unit!"

21

Brain-Drained

"Why have I been so dense?" Camden scolded herself. "Everything's been right there all along and I was just too stupid to see it. Stupid, stupid, stupid!"

She forced herself to wait until her bedside clock read 7:01. Then she slipped quietly out from under the covers and into her clothes. She knew what she had to do and time was running out.

Camden tiptoed past her parents' bedroom, down the stairs, and into the kitchen. She found Maggie on top of the dryer, snuggled warmly in the unfolded clothes.

"Wake up, Magg. We've got an important mission," Camden announced.

Maggie's eyes flicked open. She hoped it was very important, because if it wasn't, someone was going to be in big trouble for waking her up so early.

"Trust me. It's important," Camden repeated.

Maggie sat up at that. She did a quick stretch and a fast wash and was waiting by the backpack before Camden even had her jacket on. Camden tucked some tools into the pocket of her overalls. Then she held her backpack open for Maggie to climb in.

But Maggie wasn't getting into any backpack before she knew where they were going.

Camden reached out and took her cat's head in her hands. Looking Maggie straight in the eye, she said, "We have to go to WT-3's. Now, I know you don't like it there, and I promised that you'd never have to go back. But he's a thief, Maggie. He's doing something very bad that is hurting Mitch and the other kids. It could even hurt the whole world. If I don't stop him, nobody will. And I need your help."

Her cat blinked once, then climbed into the backpack without a sound. Camden gently swung the bag onto her back and stepped out of the warm kitchen into the crisp morning air.

Camden outlined her plan to Maggie as they rode down the empty streets along the ocean toward Venice.

Maggie thought it was a good plan. But she warned Camden that WT could be more dangerous than he looked.

"Oh, Maggie, I'll be fine," Camden answered. "Besides, once I tell Mitch and the others about him, they'll be on my side and he won't be able to do anything about it."

Maggie wasn't so sure.

Camden watched the early-morning surfers tame the smooth, white-crested waves. She wished she could be out there with them. Suddenly this whole thing seemed to be a huge responsibility that was too much for her to tackle.

"Well, at least I've got help," she reassured herself.

"Maw," came the instant reply.

They arrived at the (Something) View Arms sooner than Camden would have liked. She hid her bike around a corner, took a deep breath, and slipped down the stairs into the darkness of the basement. She made her way as quietly as possible through the dark, musty room. Locating the staircase, Camden slipped out the door into the dim light of the hallway.

She stopped to listen for sounds of activity, but it was much too early for the Kidsters to be there. She peeked around the corner just to make doubly sure before entering the empty lobby. Leading the way, Maggie padded silently up the stairs to the second floor. The faded bedroom doors seemed to stare forlornly at Camden as she walked quickly past them and up to the third floor. She continued through the dusty hall until she came to the rickety hodgepodge of a staircase. Maggie was already sitting at the bottom of the steps, staring up at the secret door-unit.

"Told you it was strange," she whispered to her cat.

Camden listened one more time for signs of life while Maggie sniffed the air. The fur on her back ruffled nervously; her eyes were dark with excitement.

"Okay," Camden whispered. "You stay here and keep watch for me. Remember, two meows if you hear someone coming and one meow if it's all clear."

"Meow," Maggie answered. Then she took her place as lookout on the bottom steps, ears firmly at the alert.

Camden started up the splintery steps, winding her way toward that crazy-looking door. Breathing heavily, she finally arrived at the landing on the top. Camden stared at the patchwork door. She tried to find a weak spot, some place where she could break through into the secret room beyond. The locks themselves would be too difficult to break, so she decided to work the screws out of the old latches that held the locks in place. Reaching into her overalls, Camden pulled out a short screwdriver that she had borrowed from her father's toolbox. Then she began the long process of removing the screws, one at a time. After a while she called down to Maggie.

"Meow," her cat answered promptly.

Camden went back to work, secure in the knowledge that she had a very good lookout indeed. It took her a long time to pull out all of the rusty screws and she received several splinters in the bargain. Maggie stood guard proudly, answering with a single "meow" whenever Camden called out to her.

"Finally!" Camden grumbled. She twisted the last rusty screw out and tugged the final latch away from the hinge.

The patchwork door creaked loudly as she pulled it open and peered around the corner.

"WT-3?" she called quietly. There was no response.

So Camden bravely stepped inside.

"Wow!" she exclaimed.

WT's secret room looked like the rest of the tiny rooms in the abandoned hotel, bare and dusty, with old newspapers strewn on the floor. It was exactly like all the others except for the strange glowing tube that hung in the air. Nervously, Camden took a step closer. No, it wasn't a tube. It was more like a vertical line drawn in the center of the room, and it glowed with an incredible light, a bronze light. It was as if the shining bronze sun of Camden's dream lay right behind that line and only the thinnest stream of light could sneak through. Shielding her eyes from the glare, Camden took another step closer.

"Meow! Meow!"

It was Maggie giving her the danger signal. Suddenly Camden heard the sound of WT's boots pounding down the hall below. She froze. Should she hide? No, better to get down the stairs and out of sight before he found her there. She wanted to deal with WT-3 on her own terms.

Camden slipped out the door, closing it as quickly and quietly as she could. But there was no way to hide the screws and broken latches; they would give her away. Clinging to the banister, she took the wobbly stairs two at a time. Halfway down, she heard Maggie give a warning hiss and a deep growling sound. Camden looked around but could see no sign of her cat. Then she heard a yell from WT, some scuffling, and another growl from Maggie. Suddenly they appeared from around the corner, Maggie dashing around his legs, trying to tangle up his feet and block the way.

Shouting angrily, WT stumbled down the hall toward the stairs. Camden could see that, despite Maggie's best efforts, escape was impossible. She stood tall and confronted him.

"So!" Camden announced loudly, hands firmly planted on her hips. WT stopped in his tracks. Maggie trotted to the bottom step and turned toward the enemy, hackles raised, claws ready.

WT-3 glared at Camden without a word. She had obviously taken him by surprise.

"WT-3," she said in a voice that trembled more from excitement than fear, "I know who you are!"

Without warning, he yelled furiously and came after her. But he had forgotten about Maggie. Hissing and yowling, she warned him off, claws out, ready to attack if he got any closer. Maggie knew how to fight, but she couldn't defend herself against WT's powerful kick. Camden heard his boot slam into her, knocking Maggie off the stairs and out of Camden's sight.

The sound of Maggie's painful cry brought a terrible rage to Camden. It was like a physical force that threw her down the stairs at WT. Out of control with anger, she flew at him, throwing punches. But even her desire for revenge was no match for his overwhelming strength. She screamed and bit, fought and kicked, but he tossed her aside easily. Camden flew across the hall, slamming against the wall and knocking her head painfully on the floor. She looked up just in time to see a flash of bronze hair as WT tossed his cap away and ran through his secret door.

Camden groaned, rubbing her throbbing head. She could feel the knot already growing on her forehead. She sat up and noticed a pair of dirty tennis shoes standing right next to her.

"Mitch!"

Relief washed over Camden as she leaped to her feet.

"Oh, boy," she said, shaking her head to clear it. "Am I glad to see you. WT has taken the . . ."

But she trailed off as she got a good look into the face of her friend. Mitch's eyes looked almost dead, as if the light behind them had been turned down very, very low.

"Mitch?" she whispered, trying to hold back her fear.

Then she noticed the rest of them. They were all there, staring at her with totally empty faces, just like the people on the bronze planet. Camden grabbed Mitch in a panic. She shook him violently.

"Mitch! Mitch! It's me! Camden!"

But he looked right past her.

"WT's stolen the words from your minds!" she yelled at them. "He's not from our world! Don't you see?"

She looked at her friends, desperate to make them understand. She tried The Words.

"WT is a double ungood badness! And . . . the Kidsters got brain-drain from *him*, not from grownies. He uses the power-unit to steal your thoughts and — he's a thief!" she yelled in desperation. "WT — don't you understand? WT means Word Thief! Word Thief!"

But she had absolutely no effect on them. They just stood very still, arms at their sides, completely lifeless. Camden stomped on the floor in frustration.

"Maw?"

Camden whirled around. "Maggie?"

A small gray head peered cautiously around a corner and Maggie limped slowly across the floor. Camden swept the cat up into her arms, nuzzling her face into the gray fur.

"Maggie, Maggie, Maggie," Camden murmured. "Are you all right?"

Maggie thought she'd probably survive.

Camden hugged her tightly. "Oh, I love you so much, you ol' thing!"

But Maggie pushed away and jumped to the floor. She thought maybe Camden should hurry up. That horrible WT person was getting away!

Camden took one last look at the vacant faces of her friends.

"Let's go!" she said and they took off.

Racing ahead, Maggie bounded easily up the stairs and through the door with Camden right behind her.

They barreled into the room just in time to see WT grab hold of that bright, glowing line that hung in the air. He pulled at one edge and the line began to grow wider. As Camden watched, it grew wider and wider into a rectangle and then wider still until the rectangle was the size of a small door. The bronze light was so brilliant, Camden had to shield her eyes against the glare. She could barely make out WT's tall silhouette as he stepped through the glowing door and disappeared.

"Maw?"

Camden had almost forgotten about Maggie.

"Maw?" she repeated insistently.

Camden reached down and picked up her cat. Hugging her tightly, she stared in awe at the glowing door hanging in midair. Should she follow him through into who-knows-where?

"I don't know what to do," she mumbled. "I . . . I'm scared."

Maggie didn't think this was any time to worry about things like being scared. They were either going to stop him or they weren't.

Camden gulped.

"Okay," she whispered. "If you're brave enough, then I guess I'm brave enough. Let's go."

Clutching her cat to her chest, Camden took a deep breath, closed her eyes, and stepped boldly through the shining doorway.

22

Maggie of the Great Gray Claws

THE BRONZE GLOWING LIGHT grew brighter as Camden and Maggie slipped through the mysterious doorway. Once they were inside, the shining rectangle began to close behind them until it was again only a thin vertical line in the air. The line shimmered for an instant, then began to grow shorter as if it were being erased from the bottom up. Before long, the line had become little more than a brilliant dot that flickered once and was gone.

Inside, Camden could see nothing. The light was too bright. Squinting, she looked around, trying to locate WT-3. Way off in the distance, she thought she could make out a dark shadow moving away very quickly.

"That must be him," she whispered to Maggie, whose eyes were blue slits against the glare. Very, very carefully Camden began to move in that direction. She had no idea where she was or what she was walking toward. After counting one hundred steps, Camden could see the shadowy figure pull open another door. He tugged it wider, revealing darkness on the other side, and slipped through without a backward glance. Camden began to run. The last thing she wanted was to get stuck here in never-never land. Gripping Maggie tightly, she pounded after him and threw herself through the bright doorway just as it was starting to close again.

Camden stumbled as she came through, falling heavily onto hard stone. Fortunately, Maggie leaped away in time to avoid the collision. Rubbing her bruised knee, Camden watched as the glowing door behind her closed into a thin line, which shrank to a tiny dot before it disappeared.

"I guess we'll have to find another way home," she whispered in a shaking voice.

Maggie agreed and she rubbed against Camden for reassurance.

Looking around to get her bearings, Camden noticed that she was leaning against a hard wall. She pushed away and stood up, running her hand over the smooth glass.

"I'm pleased to announce that I know exactly where we are," she told Maggie. "This is the Great Hall of Learning. I *knew* he'd come back to the bronze planet! Now we just have to find him."

Camden sounded a lot braver than she felt. She picked Maggie up and continued around the side of the huge building until she had located the doors. Luckily, there was no one in sight. Camden stared up at the enormous doors.

"No problem," she told Maggie. "Watch this."

Expecting to slide right through them the way she had

done so many times in her dream, Camden walked smack into the door, banging her head loudly against the hard surface.

"Ow!" she complained.

Maggie would have chuckled if she could have.

"That's never happened before," Camden mumbled, feeling the new lump grow on her head.

Maggie sat down to watch as Camden grunted and heaved until she had one of the huge doors open just enough for both of them to squeeze through.

"I hope Mitch and the others appreciate this," she muttered.

Inside the enormous building, Camden heard boots pounding toward them. She and Maggie both leaped behind a corner to hide.

"Word Police," Camden whispered to her cat, and they both watched the guards march noisily down the stairs. After they had gone, Camden nudged Maggie.

"Come on," she whispered and began to run lightly down the long hall.

Maggie sure hoped Camden knew where she was going.

At the end of the hall, Camden stopped in front of the Grand Classroom.

"He's in there," she said. "I just know it."

Well? Maggie wanted to know what they were waiting for.

"Okay," Camden replied, her heart pounding wildly. "Here goes nothing!"

Then she grabbed the doors and boldly flung them open.

The Grand Classroom hadn't changed since Camden saw it in her first planet dream so long ago. This time, however, it was completely deserted except for two lone figures at the front of the class. Camden could instantly feel the dark power in the room as WT-3 and the Teacher faced each other, the gray whirling cube hovering between them.

Camden recognized the familiar sparks that flew from WT's eyes into the power-unit. But from the other side, flowing out of that spinning void, Camden could see a colorful stream of vague shapes and shadowy forms. She saw blurry pictures and unclear images flowing in and out of each other like watercolors all running together. And the whole swirling stream was being sucked up into the evil eyes of the Teacher.

After a few moments Camden realized that she was watching actual thoughts made real somehow, real enough to see. That colorful stream of abstract images contained the words and ideas, the concepts and memories, of her friends back home. Stolen by WT-3 with his power-unit and his Words and his brain-wrenching Game, they were now being devoured by the greedy mind of the Teacher. Camden couldn't control the anger and outrage that rose up inside her.

"Stop that!" she yelled furiously.

Surprised, WT faltered for an instant, the sparks sputtering to a halt. Turning around, he stared at her in disbelief.

"CD-1," he stuttered.

"No!" she answered him insolently, hands on her hips. "I'm Camden Douglas and you're a thief!"

WT sneered and started to come after her, but a clawlike hand touched his shoulder, stopping him. The Teacher smiled with sinister pleasure and pointed a long, spindly finger at Camden. Camden could feel a compelling force pull at her. She fought against it, digging her heels into the ground, but the overwhelming power of the Teacher's will drew her closer and closer. Then she was face to face with that terrible presence and she felt a chill of fear creep into her heart.

The Teacher smiled again, grabbing Camden's face in a painful grip.

"Now," she boomed, "let's play The Game!" The Teacher's voice seemed to reverberate inside Camden's head and she cackled a hideous laugh that echoed through the classroom. Suddenly the twirling power-unit appeared in front of Camden's eyes and she was staring into that deep black emptiness. Struggling uselessly, Camden knew that they were going to take her thoughts too and that she was going to be left mindless, just like the rest. She forced herself to think of nothing so that the power-unit couldn't drain her of any thought or word that she held in her mind.

Nothing, nothing, nothing, she repeated over and over to herself. Nothing, nothing, nothing.

But it was impossible. Try as she might to blank out her thoughts, Camden's mind was hard at work searching for a way out of this trap. And every thought, every phrase, every word was slowly, steadily slipping away from her forever. Her vision blurred and darkened as the spinning black vacuum consumed her completely.

Suddenly, through the haze, Camden saw a sleek, gray figure leap through the air, grab the twirling power-unit, and streak away out of her sight. Released from its hold, Camden stumbled backward.

"Nooooo!" she heard WT scream.

He made a wild grab for Maggie as she sped by him with the power-unit held tightly between her jaws. Camden heard them thunder away down the long hallway and she laughed out loud with joy.

"He'll never catch her!" she declared, glaring at the Teacher victoriously. "She's much too fast!"

With a hideous scowl, her black robes flowing behind her, the Teacher advanced menacingly toward Camden. Battling her fear, Camden gritted her teeth and stood her ground. As they locked eyes, she was blasted with the full force of the Teacher's powerful will. Camden felt a shaft of ice shoot right through to her heart and she staggered backward, gasping for breath.

"I know things," the Teacher's voice rumbled. "Many things, *bad* things, about you, Camden Douglas."

And, suddenly, Camden knew she knew about all the awful things she'd ever done in her life. The Teacher knew about the doll dress that she'd stolen from her friend Patty in kindergarten and she knew about all the vegetables Camden had hidden in her napkin at the dinner table. The Teacher knew about that math test she'd cheated on; she knew about the time she had punched Hank in the stomach and she knew about all the lies Camden had been telling her parents when she wanted to go to Venice.

The Teacher chuckled. "You really are an evil little thing, aren't you?"

But way down deep inside, down in that secret, inner part of herself, Camden knew she wasn't. She'd made some mistakes and she'd done some hurtful things, but she wasn't evil. Somehow, knowing this, she felt stronger. Camden glared back at the Teacher.

"No," she replied. "You're wrong."

"Wrong?" the Teacher yelled. "Don't be ridiculous! I'm never wrong!"

"Yes, you are," Camden answered defiantly. "You have all that knowledge and you're still wrong."

The Teacher cackled again.

"And just exactly what am I wrong about?" she boomed.

Camden gulped. "You're wrong about me. I'm not evil. I'm just human."

The Teacher frowned, backing up a step. Camden could feel her dark power begin to weaken. She took a big breath and pressed on.

"And what you've done here is wrong," Camden continued bravely. "You've forced these people to give you every word, every thought, every idea they've ever had. You've taken away their hopes and their dreams! You've made them as empty as you are, and if that's not wrong then I don't know what is!"

The Teacher shook her head violently, backing up farther. She seemed to grow smaller, weaker. The black robes hung limply.

"I . . . I hate to be wrong," she stammered. "I . . . I won't be wrong! I can't be wrong!"

The Teacher stomped her feet, whimpering like a spoiled child, and for the first time Camden saw her as she really was. No longer powerful or frightening, the Teacher was nothing more than a greedy, bad-tempered woman whose search for knowledge had been twisted into a wicked thirst for power. But that power was gone now as Camden stared at her with contempt.

"You're pathetic," she said at last. "And you give teachers a bad name!"

With that, Camden turned on her heel and walked out of the Grand Classroom. Defeated, the Teacher stared after her, and somewhere inside that cold heart she knew Camden was right.

23

Just a Dream?

MARCHING BOLDLY away from the Grand Classroom, Camden spotted WT-3 standing in the middle of
the enormous hall. But he didn't look anything like the
cool, hip teenager she knew back at the (Something) View
Arms. His eyes darting this way and that, he turned in
circles, scratching his head.

"Gimme my power-unit!" he screamed at Camden.

She sighed. It had been a very long day.

"You'd better gimme it!" he whined. "Or — or — or — "

"Or what, WT?" Camden demanded. "What are you
going to do?"

He threw back an arm as if to strike her. But when she
didn't flicker an eyelash, his face crumbled, his shoulders
slumped, and he looked as if he was about to cry.

"I want my power-unit," he begged. "Please give it to
me."

She just looked at him.

"You know, WT," she said wearily, "I've just about had
enough of you and your power-units and your secret

language and your stupid Game. Now get out of my way!"

WT had no choice. Mumbling to himself, he stepped aside. Camden brushed past him without a second glance.

She found Maggie perched on a high ledge at the end of the hall, grooming herself casually. Camden smiled up at her cat.

"I told her you were too fast for him," she said.

Maggie yawned. It was really no contest. She lifted up a white paw to reveal the gray cube beneath.

Camden chuckled as Maggie daintily picked up the power-unit between sharp teeth and leaped gracefully into Camden's arms.

"Thanks for saving me back there," Camden murmured, nuzzling her face into the gray fur. "Things were looking pretty bad until you came along."

Maggie dropped the cube into Camden's palm and, snuggling close, began to purr.

Deep down in the dungeon beneath the Hall of Learning, Camden inserted the heavy key that she had found hanging on the wall into the rusty lock.

"There's just one more thing I have to do," she told Maggie, who twitched her tail impatiently.

Camden glanced around nervously even though she hadn't seen any Word Police since she left the Grand Classroom. She twisted the key and the ancient cell door creaked open.

"Professor?" Camden called quietly. She was afraid it might already be too late.

But as she stepped into the tiny cell, Camden found the old professor sitting up on his cot. He looked stronger; the color was back in his cheeks. When he glanced up, she could see that the sparkle had returned to his eyes.

"I'm Camden Douglas," she said, not quite sure where to begin. "You don't know me but, uh, I don't think that teacher's going to be giving you any more trouble."

With the help of his cane, the old gentleman slowly got to his feet. He extended a frail hand toward her.

"Nice to meet you," he replied.

Camden shook his hand carefully and glanced over at the big man and the young teacher. They were smiling.

Much later, after a long explanation and lots of questions, Camden, Maggie, the old professor, and his two friends stood outside on the steps of the Great Hall overlooking the bronze city. Down in the square, Camden was pleased to see that the people were beginning to return to normal. Released from the cruel power of the Teacher and her Word Police, the bronze-haired people were milling about in confusion, shaking their heads and rubbing their eyes.

"I'm afraid it's going to take a long time for them to relearn everything they've lost," the professor explained sadly. "But luckily" — he winked and tapped his forehead — "I've still got it all up here."

"From the looks of it," the big man added, "you've got your work cut out for you."

Alarmed, Camden looked at them.

"Are my friends going to have to start from scratch too?"

"No, don't worry," the professor answered. "That's a very powerful little object you've got there." He pointed to her pocket. "Their words are stored inside the power-unit. All you have to do is take it home and release them back to your friends."

"Release them?" Camden stammered. "Release the words? But — but . . . I don't know how to do that!"

The aged gentleman took her hand and held it gently.

"My dear, you had enough strength and will and determination to defeat the Teacher. I hardly think a little thing like a power-unit is going to be a problem."

Camden stuck her hand in her pocket and fiddled with the small cube.

"Okay," she mumbled. "If you say so."

"I say so," he answered with a twinkle in his eye.

"But I'm not quite sure how to get home," she complained. "We came here through a strange glowing line in the air."

She looked around, but there wasn't a strange glowing line anywhere in sight.

"Oh, you don't have to use the Path of Light to get home," the young woman told her.

"Path of Light?" Camden asked. "Is that what that was?"

"Of course," she answered. "You know that light travels very fast, don't you?"

Camden nodded.

"Well," she explained, "we've just found a way to hitch a ride."

"Wow!" Camden exclaimed.

"But you've got your own way home," the professor informed her.

"My own way? What do you mean?" she asked.

"How did you get here the other times?" the large man asked with his gruff voice.

Camden thought for a minute, then shook her head.

"No, no, see, that's just a dream," she explained.

Tugging at his white beard, the old professor winked at her.

"Well," he said mysteriously, "maybe it is and then again . . . maybe it isn't."

At that moment, Camden felt a cool, gentle breeze brush past her. Looking at the others with wide eyes, she laughed lightly.

"Come on, Maggie!" she called. "You're going to *love* this!"

Maggie bounded toward her. She leaped into Camden's arms just as the Star Wind swept them up and over and around into that sparkling, twinkling, wonderful starry night.

24

"Knew You Could Do It"

"WAS THAT GREAT or was that great?" Camden asked Maggie as the Star Wind blew through an open window of the (Something) View Arms, bringing them home.

Maggie, licking her ruffled fur, gave her a sideways glance. No, she did not think all that swirling and swooping was so great. In fact, she didn't like it one bit.

Camden chuckled, patting her on the head.

"You'll get used to it," she said.

Maggie's eyes darkened. Used to it? She was never going to do *that* again as long as she lived!

Camden felt for the small gray cube in her pocket.

"Come on," she said urgently. "Let's go find Mitch."

Nothing had changed much at the old hotel as Camden tumbled down the stairs into the dingy lobby. Faces empty, arms limp at their sides, Mitch and the others sat silently staring into nothingness. Looking at her friends, Camden shook her head sadly.

"I sure hope I can make this thing work," she mumbled.

Holding the power-unit in her palm, Camden crossed the fingers of her other hand. The professor had put so much trust in her. She just hoped she wouldn't let him and everybody else down.

Taking a deep breath, Camden stared into the power-unit. That was the only thing she could think of to do. Concentrating as hard as she could, she poured every ounce of her energy into that tiny cube. Straining with the effort, she willed the power-unit to move.

"Come on, you thing," she grumbled. "Come on!"

Just when she didn't think she had anything left, Camden made one last wild thrust, throwing all of her strength of mind into the power-unit.

"Come on!" she gasped. "I want my friends back. Now *move*!"

And it moved. Slowly at first, then gradually picking up speed, the cube turned. Camden wanted to cheer but the spinning cube took all of her concentration. Faster and faster it twirled until the cube became a whirling vacuum, a deep black void that held enormous power in its dark depths.

"Release them!" Camden commanded, gulping for air. "Release the words! Let them go! Do it, *now*!"

And suddenly the lobby was filled with a sweeping rainbow of colorful forms, vague shapes, and shadowy images. The very real thoughts and ideas, visions and dreams, hopes and fantasies of Camden's long-lost friends flew out of the darkness back into their hearts and minds.

Of course, some of their thoughts would be lost forever. Those that Camden saw being sucked into the greedy mind of the Teacher were gone. There was no way to bring them back. Her friends would be able to relearn all the words, the way Camden had. But there would always be a little something missing, a momentary gap here and there or a slight glimmer of a lost idea that would be a permanent reminder of that astonishing summer.

Camden glanced over at her friends. Their faces began to grow brighter. The light returned to their eyes. Color came back to their cheeks. Grinning broadly, she held her concentration until the last of the colorful images flew out of the twirling cube and the power-unit spun to a stop.

"Hurray!" she shouted, jumping up and down.

Looking around, Camden was delighted to see all those special things that made up the faces of her friends. Danny blushed when she looked at him. Nancy's tan seemed to grow darker. She was even glad to see Hank's unfriendly scowl. But best of all, that smart, funny, wry look was back in Mitch's eyes. He winked at her.

"Welcome back," she said with a catch in her voice.

And she couldn't help it. She just had to give him a hug.

"So, you see, The Game was a way for WT to confuse us," Camden explained to them later. "He twisted our thinking and knocked a hole in the way that we thought the world was supposed to be. He made us go through all of those weird experiences so he could sneak in and steal the words out of our heads. And he replaced the ones he'd stolen with that slang of his so we wouldn't notice until it was too late. He was a thief, you know, just a common, ordinary everyday thief."

"You can say that again," Nancy added, rubbing her eyes. "Everything was off. I couldn't think straight. I couldn't talk. The only thing I cared about was that dumb Game."

"Right," Camden continued. "And he turned us against our parents so we wouldn't go to them for help."

"What a creep," Mark commented sourly.

"A double ungood mondo-creep," Danny added.

Somebody threw a sneaker at him, and soon they were all laughing again as if this were a perfectly normal day at the end of summer.

"Knew you could do it," Mitch said, nudging her with an elbow.

"What?" Camden asked, looking up at him.

"I knew you could do it," he repeated and plopped down next to her on the floor. "I couldn't read anymore. I didn't care about anything. I hated almost everyone. Something *had* to be wrong."

"Is that why you voted against me?" she asked. " 'Cause that really hurt my feelings, you know."

"Sorry, kiddo, but it had to be done. I was counting on you to figure it out," he explained. "Are you mad?"

He peered at her through his glasses.

"I guess not," Camden answered with a shrug. "But how did you know about the planet and everything?"

He stared at her with a blank expression.

"Planet? What planet?" he asked.

Camden chuckled.

"Never mind," she answered with a secret smile. She would tell him all about it . . . someday.

At home that night, after an energetic game of Scrabble that Camden almost won, she presented Maggie with her reward.

"Thanks, Magg," Camden said, pouring a whole bag of Fritos into her yellow bowl. "I never could have done it without you. You're the greatest cat ever!"

But Maggie already knew that.

Lying in bed later, Camden stared up at the ceiling, her cat curled into a warm ball at her feet. She thought about the bronze planet and she already missed the old professor with his tattered brown hat. She missed the gentle young woman and the big man with his gravelly voice. She hadn't even had a chance to say good-bye.

Camden reached over and picked up the power-unit from her bedside table. Turning it over and over in her hand, she wondered if it still held any mysteries. It was probably just a lifeless, dull gray cube now, nothing more than a souvenir of her great adventure. Camden sighed and put it back, then snuggled down under the covers.

Suddenly she sat up again, eyes wide.

"But if he was WT-3," she muttered softly, "then where are WT-1 and WT-2?"

Camden groaned, pulling the covers up over her head. She didn't want to think about it.